A Place Without Heroes

BENISON CHRISTOPHER

A Place Without Heroes

ISBN: 978-1-0686500-0-0

Published by
Black Writing Publishers
www.blackwritingpublishers.com
info@blackwritingpublishers.com
blackwritingpublishers@gmail.com
51 Meath Street
Middlesbrough
TS1 4RS
North Yorkshire
North East England
United Kingdom

Credits:
Editor: Black Tower Publishers
Cover: Wola Thomas

DEDICATION

To everyone who needs a hero.

This collection of short stories is a marvellous manifestation of the functions of enlightening and delighting the reader in the tradition of the Horatian concept of "UTILE ET. DULCE." The incidents in the stories reflect the instructive contradictory nature of life in the society they portray. The narration of the stories is made delightful by being garnished with breathtaking suspense, memorable flashbacks, metaphysical similes, and fascinating proverbs employed in the tradition of Chinua Achebe's narrative use of that technique.

Professor Emeritus Romanus Egudu.

FOREWORD

In your hands, you hold a delightful compilation of short stories that will captivate you from the first page to the last. Each narrative within these pages is masterfully written, weaving together engaging plots and compelling characters that will draw you in and leave a lasting impression.

The decision to open this collection with "The Perfect Husband" is a stroke of genius. This story sets the tone for the entire book with its intriguing plot and well-crafted characters. From the outset, the setting is skillfully established, immersing you immediately in the world the author has created. The suspense and emotional depth of "The Perfect Husband" make it an excellent introduction, ensuring that you are hooked from the very beginning.

Equally impressive is the choice to conclude the collection with "The Riverbank." This story provides a fitting end, leaving you with a sense of satisfaction and reflection. "The Riverbank" beautifully ties together the themes explored in the previous stories, and its poignant ending resonates deeply, making it a memorable finish to this exceptional collection.

The diversity in themes and settings throughout these stories keeps you engaged, while the consistent quality of writing ensures a cohesive and enjoyable reading experience. Prepare to be immersed in a world of stories that will linger with you long after you turn the final page.

STORIES

The Perfect Husband..1
Being with a Fat Girl..33
A Place Without Heroes..51
The Weeds..85
The Pastor and the Robber..103
The Fear of Darkness...115
The Riverbank...131

The Perfect Husband

"Woman, tell us again, how did your husband die?" One of the seven-man panel of elders from the Osaretin family asked Ireti.

She was supposed to be quivering as she knelt, head-shaven, and draped in white *iro* and *buba* before the panel, but she tried to stay strong.

"Woman, did you not hear him?" another asked, shoving his Android phone threateningly in her face.

Ireti turned her head towards him and rested her eyes on his neck. It was the most extended neck she had ever seen. His neck stretched tall like the trunk of a tree, bearing the weight of an Adam's apple as large as a ripe melon. It throbbed each time he spoke or swallowed saliva, which happened a lot. Despite her situation, Ireti could not help paying it a little more attention. She was as fascinated as she was the first time she saw an ostrich. Another thing that caught her eye was the Android phone the man kept pushing in her face, as if he meant to pluck out her eyes with it. She had bought him the phone a lifetime ago when she thought he was a human being, never knowing it would one day become a weapon in the hands of her enemy. She shook her head in pity.

"Ireti!" Pa Ozua, the eldest among them, called. "Did you not hear what they asked you? Tell us how exactly your husband died."

"But I have told the story many times already, sir," she replied.

"Yes, we know that you have told us the story many times already, but the matter at hand is a very grave one. Obigho Osaretin was a very great man. The greatest of us all. We, therefore, can never be bored by the story of how such a great iroko was cut down from the roots. Please tell us again."

"Like I have said several times already, we went out that night for dinner—"

"Ehen! 'We' meaning you and him, or you, him, and your imbecile daughter?" the ostrich interjected, his Adam's apple moving up and down his long neck.

"I, him, and our beautiful daughter," Ireti replied.

She hated it so much when people implied behind her back that her daughter was an imbecile, let alone when they voiced it to her hearing or to her face.

Ireti looked at the ostrich scornfully, hoping he would choke on his own saliva. However, that did not happen because he asked, "Why did you people go out for dinner again? Is it that you cannot cook or what?"

She shook her head. It was not his fault. Why would he not ask her dirty questions when she was clad in plain white clothes, had no shoes on, had her head shaven, and was kneeling before him? Why would he not have the courage to ask her utterly stupid questions? Those days—the days before her husband's demise when Uncle Oberure visited with his *long-throat*, magically devouring almost anything and everything in sight into his tiny stomach—he used to worship the ground she walked on. Now, she was on the ground. Why would he not trample on her?

"Sir, I can cook, but Obigho liked to have family dinners outside once in a while."

"Obigho? Obigho? Is that how you call his name without any form of respect?" he asked.

"I am sorry, sir. What I mean to say is that I can cook, but my husband liked to have family dinners outside once in a while."

"Once in a while or all the time? You know I used to frequent your house in those days. I never saw you enter the kitchen. It was always from one fast food joint to the next. Either that or you hire a very expensive cook to handle your kitchen business even though you were a mere housewife. So, what exactly was your work in that house if you could not cook our son's meals?"

Uncle Oberure was her husband's only surviving brother; Ireti, therefore, could not understand why he would say 'our son' instead of 'my brother.' Indeed, the wasp has undoubtedly become a hawk.

"It was my husband who insisted that..."

"That what? That you squander all of his money on exotic meals cooked by others when your hands are not broken?" Uncle Oberue asked. "Is that why there was no money in his bank accounts after his death?"

The others started to murmur. Ireti remained mute.

Uncle Oberure turned to the others. "You all saw the statement of accounts she brought, right? When you add all the figures together, the money is not even up to five hundred thousand naira. How much was it again? Was it not four hundred and twenty-two thousand naira that this woman claimed our brother had in all his five bank accounts?"

The others nodded in affirmation.

"Me, I know Obigho used to talk about a Union Bank account those days, but this woman has sworn that there is no Union Bank account. She even swore on the life of her imbecile daughter that she brought statements for all the accounts she knew about. I know Obigho to be the perfect husband—a man too good and kind, to a fault. A man who told his wife everything about himself and never hid anything from her. What sort of man does not know how to keep a secret? I used to tease him. So, this woman can't even say our son hid any bank accounts from her."

"No, he never hid any bank accounts from me—"

"Ehen! Ehen! So why isn't his Union Bank account statement here? Or is that where you're hiding all his money after killing him in cold blood?" he accused.

She had no answer, or rather, her answer would be too heavy, so she stayed mute.

"Continue your story," Uncle Obe, as she used to call him, said. "Tell us exactly how he died. Make sure you don't leave anything out."

"As I was saying," she wanted to add 'before the hungry fowl interrupted me,' "my husband, our daughter, and I went out on the evening of his death for a family dinner. We returned to the house a little past nine in the evening. My husband went into the shower for a bath as soon as we got in—"

"Which shower did he use?" Uncle Osahon interrupted. "We know you people lived in a mansion filled with many toilets and shower rooms."

"He used the main shower attached to the master's bedroom."

"While he showered, where were you?" Uncle Osahon asked again.

"I went to our daughter's room to give her a bath before—"

"How old is your daughter again?" the eldest, Pa Ozua, asked.

"She is fifteen, sir."

"Fifteen? Fifteen years old, and you still give her a bath?" he asked again.

"Oho! You haven't seen her? She's a vegetable o, an imbecile, never knowing which shoe should go on which leg. In fact, she cannot even control her own legs," Uncle Obe mocked.

"Rich people and their many curses!" Pa Ozua teased.

The others laughed, except Ireti. She was so upset that the heat of her anger could have burned them all!

"I remember fifteen years ago when I attended the girl's naming ceremony," Uncle Oberue began. "Obigho and this woman here wore matching attire. They danced like silly children. Little did we know they were celebrating the birth of a dead child!"

Everyone, including the big cashew tree they sat under, laughed thunderously, except Ireti.

She continued her narration as soon as they were done laughing—the laughter that could have cost them their heads if Ireti had had her way. "After bathing our daughter, I was trying to put her to sleep when I heard a loud scream from our room. I ran to the room to find my husband clutching his chest and bleeding from his mouth and nose."

All the men started to make sad noises, hugging themselves tightly like they were hearing the story for the first time.

Ireti ignored them and continued her story. "I immediately called the family doctor who came to examine him, but before—"

"You mean you called the family doctor after you killed him with your witchcraft?" Uncle Obe asked, still hugging himself tightly and shaking his head exaggeratedly, feeling quite sorry for the dead. "Everyone here knows that when a man dies in the manner that Obigho did, it is nothing but witchcraft!"

"Actually, the doctor said he suffered a massive heart attack."

"Why will he not suffer a massive heart attack with a witch like you for a wife who has been eating up all his seeds?" Pa Odion, who was Pa Ozua's younger brother, asked. "Or is it not true you eat up your children only two days after their birth?"

"Yes!" the other men chorused.

"Seven children! Seven children!" said Pa Odion. "This evil woman has buried seven of our son's seeds! Six of them died mysteriously two days after their birth. The seventh died on his fifth birthday!" He turned to the others. "Or my kinsmen, have I mixed up the story?"

"No o!" they all chorused.

"In fact, you left out the part where she ate some of them growing in her womb before they could see the light of day." Uncle Obe added.

Ireti shook her head sorrowfully. A lion was only as feared as it could roar. If anything took away its roar, then even ants and maggots would command more respect.

Pa Odion cleared his throat. "Ireti," he said. "Aside from your imbecile daughter, who was in the house with you that can corroborate your story?"

"No one else, sir."

"No one else? Did I not hear that you people lived with so many servants? Did you not have one to wipe your buttocks clean after you defecate in the toilet and another to brush your teeth after every meal?" he further quizzed.

"I sent them on a vacation during that time so we could enjoy quality time toge—"

"You mean you sent them all away?" Uncle Obe cut in. "I told you all, this evil woman killed our son! Oh, Obigho! Obigho! What sort of fate has befallen you so? I told you all that this woman deserves nothing but death! An eye for an eye! A tooth for a tooth! How is it possible that she so conveniently sent all the domestic staff out of the house just about the time our son died? I say she killed him for his wealth!"

Ireti could see the others lapping up every word that came out of Uncle Obe's mouth, but that was their bloody business. She had told her story and was prepared to stick to it, even if she had a noose around her neck. In fact, what pissed her off the most was how Uncle Obe kept referring to her late husband as 'our son'. Was Obe not only his older brother again? The two of them were just a couple of years apart. She only referred to him as Uncle Obe because she was told that a woman must never call her in-laws by their names as a mark of respect.

"Ireti, is it true you killed your husband?" Pa Ozua asked with the sternest look she had ever seen.

Ireti tossed the question around in her head and figured that a fish could only get caught once it opened its mouth. It was always better not to be quoted verbatim by your enemies when you could afford it, so she stayed mute.

"Ireti? Did you not hear the question? Is it that your ears have become deaf or that your lips have become glued?" Pa Odion asked.

"Were you people expecting a reply?" Uncle Obe added. "Were you expecting this hardened witch to confess to her witchcraft so easily? This evil woman killed poor Obigho for his money despite how kind he was to her!" He jumped off his seat, moved closer to Ireti, and landed two deafening slaps on either side of her cheeks, shouting. "What? What didn't Obigho do for you? How many men did you see pamper their wives like Obigho pampered you? Ha! Obigho! I warned you not to marry this Yoruba witch, but you didn't listen! I also warned you that when you pamper a woman silly like you did this evil witch here, you thrust daggers in her hands to stab your soul with," he lamented in tears.

"Take heart, Oberure," Pa Ozua consoled. "What is dead cannot be undead, but if she had a hand in his death, his spirit would bring her to book. She has beaten the fiery drums; she should prepare to dance the dance of shame until life is snuffed out of her."

"Hmmm! What worries me the most is the news I received from the city about how, in less than a month since our son died, his business disappeared like water drying up under the scorching sun. Hmmm! Ireti, explain to us what happened to his business," Uncle Obe said. "How did you manage to sink his business empire to the ground in just one month?"

"I don't know what happened to the business. My husband always managed things himself."

"Of course he did! And, of course, you don't know what happened to the business! How would you know when all you did day after day was paint your face like a Calabar masquerade and order Chinese by the hour?" Uncle Obe intended to bite more than he could chew.

"So, Ireti, you mean to tell us all that what's left of our son is only one building—the one at Maitama, Abuja, where you people lived; two cars—one he drove until his death and one rickety one you salvaged from your maiden home; and a paltry sum in the bank?" Pa Ozua asked.

"That is correct, sir," Ireti replied.

"That cannot be true!" Uncle Obe disagreed. He turned to the others and said, "Our son was too wealthy for that to be all that remains of him. Obigho, who dined at the same table as Dangote, reduced to this? There must be more to this than meets the eye!"

"I swear, I am very convinced that this woman sold all of our brother's property and stole all of his money before she killed him with witchcraft." Pa Odion said.

"Ireti, you brought your husband's bank statements like we requested. What about your own bank statements?" Pa Ozua asked.

Ireti dug into the folds of her wrapper, brought out some neatly folded papers, and laid them at their feet. Uncle Obe picked them up and examined them.

"You see what I have been telling you people?" Uncle Obe asked. "How did this woman know we would ask for her own bank statement if she isn't a witch? And look what she brought! Only two accounts! How can the wife of a multi-billionaire have only two bank accounts? The worst part is the amount in the accounts. The GTB account has only fifty-six thousand, two hundred and forty-nine naira, and twenty-four kobo, while the First Bank account has only thirty-two thousand, eight hundred and fourteen naira, and ten kobo! Less than a hundred thousand naira! This woman is not just a bloody killer but a bloody thief and a liar, too!"

"Maybe you should hand me over to the police," Ireti began to say, before a resounding slap from Uncle Obe sealed her lips.

The way the slap shook even the cashew tree, the others expected Ireti to wince in pain and even cry, but she was not about to let the maggots see her pain or tears.

"Look at her! She can't even cry! I have never seen a woman who lost her husband so defiant!" Pa Oyegun said. "Since this woman stepped foot in Benin, I have not seen her shed a tear for our lost son! Abomination!" He spat.

"How can she have a tear for someone whose life she stole?" Uncle Obe asked.

"We warned our son when he said it was a foreign woman from Yorubaland he wanted to marry," Pa Oyegun said. "We told him not to try it, but he said it was either her or no one else. He was most certainly blown away by her strange beauty, not knowing she was a beautiful serpent. Look how he ended: rich while alive, poor in death, with no one to carry on his legacy! There have been many attempts to have a child, yet there is nothing to show for it. His widow cannot even cry over him." He shook his head in pity.

"Okay, you say you have brought papers showing all you and our son own. What about the ones people have been sending to you since he died? I am very sure that a man as wealthy as our son was would have had a lot of rich friends who would have been sending you millions now that he's dead. So, where's all the money they've been sending you?" Pa Odion asked.

Uncle Obe's Adam's apple bulged, waiting for her reply.

"Yes, it is true. I received some money from his friends and associates—"

"Ehen? Ehen? So where is it?" Uncle Obe asked impatiently.

"It was what we used for the burial," Ireti said flatly.

"You, this woman, are just a bloody liar! How much did we spend during the burial to have consumed all you got from his friends and associates?"

The bastard! Ireti fumed.

It had only been a week since the burial, and the idiot had already forgotten that he was the one who convinced the other family members that they should kill one cow each to celebrate each year their illustrious son lived on earth. Fifty cows were slaughtered in total, yet no kobo came from any of them. They said they wanted their son laid in the most gorgeous of caskets, a befitting gold-plated one. She gave them an arm and a leg for the purchase, yet all she saw during the burial was a bland wooden casket. She gave money for costly wreaths, yet only hungry-looking flowers were supplied on the burial morning. She gave them money for musicians from the East to give the occasion some colour 'so their respectable guests would not be disappointed'. She gave money for the twenty-page list of items they claimed were for the funeral rites. Then, she also gave a few more million as a fine for not coming 'home' as often as she should have. She also bought expensive matching lace fabrics for all the family members to wear to the funeral, including all their nose-dripping bastard children.

It was only a week ago, and they had forgotten how lavishly they spent!

"Sir, I did not keep any records of the amount spent. You know I have been in mourning and was not allowed out of the house. I brought all the money I received to the village. As we speak, only a thousand naira is left." She loosened the folds of her wrapper, untied the edge, brought out a crumpled one thousand naira note, and placed it at their feet. Uncle Obe dived at the note.

Pa Ozua cleared his throat. "After listening to all the deliberations, we have decided that you must remain in the village until we can determine that you did not have a hand in our son's death. You will, therefore, be here for at least the customary one-year mourning period, after which you may return to the city if you so wish, should we find you innocent of all charges. But knowing what we feel in our hearts and given the funeral fortification performed on our son before he was laid in the ground, we are convinced that you will not last a month in this village. Obigho was a strong man when he lived, and we have armed him to be a fiercer warrior in death, so be prepared! You shall give the keys to the Maitama mansion to Oberure, who will see to it that wall geckos do not overrun the place before your return... if you return! But before then, you shall go to the bank with him tomorrow morning, Monday, where you must put his phone number to receive your bank alerts. That way, we can better manage whatever funds come in from the friends of our late son."

Ireti could hear Uncle Obe speaking through Pa Ozua because, really, what was an old village man's business with banks and alerts?

All of that happened four months ago. It had been four months of Ireti daring the spirit of her late husband to come after her—four months of doing nothing but go over her life with her darling husband. Sometimes, she relived the beautiful times they shared: from the day they met at a mutual friend's birthday party, to the day he proposed by the poolside at the Agura Hotel, and their grand wedding in Dubai.

"Ireti, a woman as beautiful and delicate as you deserves a super-rich husband who can provide her with all the good things of life," he told her on their wedding night.

"But you are super-rich, and you already provide me with the good things of life," she replied, stroking his nose teasingly.

"There's nothing super-rich about being a bank manager in a country as frustrating as Nigeria. But all that is going to change soon. I am going to be super, super rich for you and our children to come. Seeing as I can never be as rich as you deserve as a mere bank manager, I have decided to quit my job and go into imports and exports."

"Quit your job?" Ireti was alarmed. It was not the kind of conversation she expected to have on her wedding night.

"Yes, my darling. You just need to trust me, okay?" he said, kissing her lips tenderly.

"I trust you, but you know I just got out of school. Why don't you wait for me to get a job first before you quit, or at least give the business time to pick up?"

"Nah! You seem not to know how extraordinarily beautiful you are. Your type should never have to work. I don't want you to ruin your very delicate hands. All you have to do as my wife is stay pretty all day and give me children as beautiful as you. Leave the rest for me to handle, okay?"

And so, her fairytale life began. "The dream life," as her friends called it. She and Obigho were the perfect couple, always holding hands and sharing jokes whenever they were together. The cherry on the cake came when they had their first daughter, Abieyuwa, a sheer joy to behold. Beautiful! Just like her mother! Sadly, after her, no other child wanted to stay with the couple.

Two days after birth, Ireti would wake to find her bundles of joy ice-cold with blood caked in their nostrils and mouths. Even more disheartening was when they started to see the signs clearly when Abieyuwa turned five. At age five, she could scarcely hold her head up. She had no social smile and could not make more than one syllabic word a few times per day. No matter how hard anyone tried, her upper and lower lips became estranged friends that must never meet. Ireti noticed that she drooled a lot when she was just a few months old, but she dismissed it as a teething sign. It was now apparent that something was wrong with their precious child. They had carried her from hospital to hospital for a while until they resigned themselves to fate.

Despite their challenges, Ireti and her husband remained glued together in love. Ireti had a tough time dealing with the loss of their children and the sad fate that befell their only child, but Obigho remained a sturdy shoulder to cry and lean on.

Obigho kept his promise of becoming super-rich because shortly after the birth of Abieyuwa, he became wealthy enough to rent an apartment in Asokoro, a highbrow area in Abuja. He even got her a new car just to say, "Thank you." The fact that she lost the other children did not stop him from getting her a new car for every child she pushed out. Ireti felt guilty about accepting the gifts when the children did not stay, but Obigho told her not to worry and promised her that they would soon have one who would stay. And he was right! Their fourth child stayed; he bore Obigho's name, but Obigho refused to be the boy's father, which was all Ireti's fault.

During their conversation on their wedding night, Obigho emphasised that, according to the tradition of his people, it was tremendously vital that he bury his children's placenta. That night, he stressed that a child did not belong to the father if the father did not bury the placenta that gave the child life. So, Ireti always gave him the placenta of all their children.

But Ehimwenma came a little early while his father was on a business trip. She usually would tell the attending nurse to save the placenta for her, but this time, she was too in love with Ehi and too anxious for his wellbeing to remember such a silly thing as protecting his placenta. In truth, she always considered the placenta business to be a ridiculous thing, but it had nearly cost her her picture-perfect marriage.

As soon as Obigho returned from his trip, which he 'cut short to be by her side', she rushed into his arms, weeping, happy that her best friend had finally come to pray with her for the safety of their son, who was in the ICU as he had complications at birth.

"I hope you kept the placenta," were the first words that tumbled from his mouth.

"Oh my God! I completely forgot!"

"What do you mean you completely forgot?"

"We changed hospitals after birth, my love. I must have left it at the first hospital. It has been days already. I believe they must have trashed it by now." Ireti did a quick calculation! "Wow! It's been days already, sweetie! Four days! And our son is still alive!" She gave her husband a weary, broad smile, but he did not smile back.

"The one time you're giving me a living child after a very long time—a son for that matter—you just had to ruin it all by denying me the honour of burying his placenta, thereby denying me my place as his father! You just had to turn our joy into mourning yet again!" With that, he stormed out of the hospital room and never returned home again until the boy was four months old.

Ireti could not understand it. What sort of tradition places so much emphasis on waste products like the placenta? Placenta that some people use for *suya* in some parts of the world? Placenta that some people use for arts and crafts? Placenta that some others throw away as garbage? Her whole life and happiness were now wrapped around the little thing. Try as she may, she could never understand it!

Even when Obigho returned home, it took a few more months for him to completely forgive her for her carelessness and for things to return to how they used to be, but he refused to be responsible for the child in any way. Thankfully, he still never spared his wife anything. From what she got for herself and Abieyuwa, she saved for their son's school fees and upkeep. He remained a loving and devoted husband, but only when Ehimwenma was out of sight. Ireti loved her husband nonetheless, and she prayed he would come around to accept their little boy as his someday, placenta tradition or not.

Four more times, she got pregnant, and four more times, she laid casket upon casket. The two who lived brought her immense joy and satisfaction. Still, her eyes lost their sparkle over the years, and her laughter became humourless.

Obigho remained a generous lover, showering her with the latest edition of her favourite cars with each child she lost—anything to cheer up his girl. He bought the mansion they lived in at Maitama in her name and took her to exotic places, where he would thoroughly lavish money on her and their beautiful but 'broken' child. They took pictures hand in hand at all the lovely places they visited together. Every day, he dropped a few lines of poetry on all her social media pages, singing how wonderful she was and how exceptionally lucky he was to have her, to the envy of her friends, many of whom hated their own husbands for 'not being as perfect as Obigho'. Their tale was as captivating as a river winding through the savannah until it cascaded down rocky slopes.

You see, Obigho usually bathed their daughter every fortnight, right from when she was five years old, without a miss. He called it 'father-daughter bonding time'. He would take them all out for a nice dinner, all of them but Ehimwenma, who still got no affection from his father. After dinner, he would tell his wife to go shower in preparation for him while he bathed their daughter and tucked her in for the night.

Over the years, it became a ritual until one of those nights when she could not wait to share with him the joy, sadness, and anxiety of expecting yet another child. As soon as she dropped the call from their family doctor, just after he gave her the good news, she ran with trembling feet towards the door leading to their daughter's room, only to stop mid-track as she heard strange yet familiar sounds. She knew what she heard but wanted her eyes to be witnesses for her ears, so she decided to look through the keyhole. It was a decision that changed all their lives forever!

Ireti found her legs after what seemed like an eternity; she found her legs, but they were as heavy as rain-soaked logs. She only had the will to move them back into her matrimonial room when everything became still. Then, she tiptoed to their bedroom and held her stomach, writhing in pain and hoping her husband would not see beyond her charade.

Fortunately, Obigho travelled the following morning and was not due back for a fortnight. As soon as he stepped out the door, she sent all the domestic staff on holiday, packed up her children to her friend, Tinuke's house, and implored her to travel out of the state with them until she told her to bring them back. She also vowed never to tell anyone what was going on. Next, she hired a technician to install a hidden camera just by the safe where Obigho kept all his money. Obigho shared everything with her, but not the safe's combination, and she had often wondered why he never kept money in the bank. It all made sense now.

Oh! Abieyuwa! How could her daughter ever forgive her for being so negligent? Would she ever forgive her for failing her as a mother?

She remembered now the sad look the girl wore every fortnight and how her eyes were always so sad, like she was trying to tell her something, but her gaping mouth could never hold the words firmly enough for them to make any sense. Because the girl had unique health challenges, she dismissed all the warning signs as just symptoms of her existing issues. Ireti had wept for days as her life for the past sixteen years started to flash before her eyes in technicolour.

She understood then what Obigho was trying to do on Ehimwenma's fifth birthday when she walked in on him virtually naked in their son's room, save for the red cloth wrapped around his waist. He had been trying to put a red mark on the boy's forehead when she walked in on them. At first, she was shocked and confused, but Obigho gave her a charming smile and dismissed her concerns with a wave, saying that he and the boy were playing a little game. She then remembered that the boy was sleeping after the exhausting birthday celebration she had single-handedly organised. How could a sleeping child play games? How stupid could anyone be? She remembered then how the boy started running a temperature that night; his body felt so hot as if he were placed over burning coals. She remembered how she had prayed for the little boy that night until her sweat became as thick as blood. Yet she never suspected something so sinister was happening right beneath her nose. She hated herself; she hated herself so much for being so blind and trusting and for not protecting any of her children enough, both the living and the dead.

Fortunately, the boy lived. What she did not know at the time was that Obigho had told all his family members that their boy had died on his fifth birthday. No wonder he always ensured the boy was well tucked away whenever any of his family members visited. Suddenly, the mansion started to spin underneath her feet, and it hit her hard in the face that everything in the house had been purchased with her children's lives! She ran out to the garage, and there they were—all the cars Obigho got her for each child she lost—each one more expensive than the last. Oh! Her children! She held her womb, weeping! She knew her children, all by their names; they still came to her in her dreams. How could she have known that when she drove around in the Mercedes S Class jesting with her envious friends, it was Abieyuwa's health she was riding in? How could she have known that Efosa was the G-Wagon, Eghosa was the Bentley, Uyi was the Rolls-Royce Ghost, Omosigho was the Ferrari, Abioye was the Lamborghini Aventador, and Obose was the Bugatti Chiron? How could she have been so blind and stupid? She kept asking herself.

Each day she waited for her husband to return brought new insight and revelation. She went over every day of the last sixteen years of her marriage until she nearly ran mad. Now, she clearly saw the importance of the placenta he craved each time she had a child. She had handed him the placenta bags, consequently handing him their children's spirits. All the luxury she ever enjoyed with him had come through nine months of overwhelming discomfort and days of excruciating pain in the labour room, several times over! Every penny they owned, the fine sheets they slept on, the expensive meals they ate—everything was bought with the blood of their children! She knew she could never forgive herself, but it was time to make things right.

The evening before Obigho's arrival, she went to the local market and bought several sets of knives. She could not sleep that night; she sat on the kitchen floor, naked as the day she was born, sharpening and re-sharpening the knives. She did not stop; she could not stop until the following day, just a few hours before her husband walked in. She knew the routine well. He would walk in, swing her around in his arms, kiss her, give her presents, dash into their bathroom for a quick bath, and then ask to take her and their daughter to a lovely dinner. She was ready for the show! And just like she predicted, he came in and swung her around in his arms. He kissed her, and she kissed him back. She received her presents with thanks and waited as he returned from the bathroom and got dressed.

"Where's everyone? The whole place is awfully quiet," he complained as soon as he returned.

"Oh, I sent the staff on a short holiday so we could have some alone time together," she said, smiling sweetly.

"You sent them on a holiday? Wait a minute! Where's Abieyuwa?" he asked.

Ireti heard the distress in his voice. "I sent her to my mother's place for a brief stay," she answered flatly.

"You did what?! With whose consent?"

"I didn't think it was that big a deal," she said as she watched his eyes suddenly turn icy red.

"What exactly do you mean by it's not that big a deal? Are you unaware that we usually go out for dinner when I return from my trips, after which I'll spend some time with my daughter? You'll go and get her back this very minute!"

"I won't!" she said defiantly, getting off the sofa to quickly lead the conversation to the bedroom where she had buried the knives under their bed.

A punch in the face sent her reeling before she could reach the staircase.

"You dare speak to your husband in such a manner? How dare you?!" His voice suddenly had the power of a thousand men.

Within the blink of an eye, he became a stranger, and once he started to hit her across the face, he could not stop. Shock and unbelief swept through Ireti's body; except for his rage over the placenta she failed to preserve, Obigho had never as much as said an unkind word to her before.

"I... I... I... am..." she stammered, trying to tell him she was pregnant, but the punches obstructed the words.

She must have passed out because, when she opened her eyes again, she was chained like a dog to one of the floor lamps in the living room.

"I just returned from your mother's at Lugbe. She said she has not seen Abieyuwa since the last time she was here, about a year ago! Woman! Where is my daughter?"

Ireti had wanted to spill the beans and let it all out, but something about his desperation made her resolve to see how the story would end.

"I don't know where she is," she gasped, trying to fully regain consciousness.

She was really exhausted and in great pain, but she had endured the worst kind of pain over the years—the pain of birthing children only to lose them to death. Nothing now, not even death, was going to make her allow her daughter to be defiled by her father again!

"You don't know where she is? You don't know where she is! Hold on a second. I'll refresh your memory!" He quickly unfastened the Gucci belt that held his Armani pants in place and started to thrash her blindly with it. "Where is my daughter?" he yelled as he whipped her to his heart's content.

He whipped her until the black, lacy gown she was wearing became as heavy as a concrete slab, wrapped up in her own blood. The only thing Ireti worried about as he whipped her was her unborn child. Several times, she tried to reason with the monster her sweet husband had become, but her sixth sense told her there was no way to reason with a desperate beast. In fact, if he knew of the pregnancy, he might just divert all his energies towards her stomach and force her to choose between the children she already had and the one she was yet to have. She, therefore, forced her mind to see past the moment and focus on a time when she would have conquered her husband, the beast! Whatever it was, she knew she had to win!

'When there is too much to lose, winning is the only option!' she told herself. The how-to was what she still needed to learn.

As Obigho's strength drained and Ireti remained unbending, he unchained her, grabbed her by the hair, and dragged her on her back up and down the staircase. It was midway through the third trip that it occurred to him that if he killed her, he might never know where Abieyuwa was. So, he stopped, chained her back to the floor lamp, and whisked out of the house, not to return until two days later.

After Obigho left the house with his insanity, Ireti was filled with enormous bitterness towards him for what he had just done to her and what he had done over the years. The only thing that could soothe her nerves now was his head dripping on a silver platter! If only she could reach for the sharpened knives upstairs in their room.

She tried to pull her weight up the stairs, but it was an impossible thing to do. She was too weak. Then there was the problem of pulling the floor lamp up, too. The floor lamp, one of four that looked exactly alike, was one of the costliest things in their living room. They were custom-made in China; they were taller than she was and were twice her weight—some of the very irrelevant vain things Obigho spent money on. They were irrelevant because, despite costing an arm and a leg, no bulb could stay on in them beyond five minutes, and all efforts to get them working proved abortive. Yet, the company that made them swore it was their best work yet. Ireti had advised that they return the useless things to the company, but Obigho insisted they keep them for their aesthetic value. She could not quite remember which of her children died to ship the useless pieces home now, but being alone in the massive building, a prisoner in her own home, gave her ample time to look around their living room. It was filled with vain things they did not have much use for, from the unbelievably costly Italian chairs to the pricey paintings on the wall and the massive chandelier looming over her head.

The chandelier! She remembered it was bought around the time she got the Ferrari, meaning it was Omosigho who towered over her, illuminating the entire living room all by herself!

Ireti tried to reach for the stairs again. And again, she failed. She wanted nothing more in this life than to go up the stairs, get into their room, and grab the knives she had spent so much time sharpening. Obigho had caught her unawares this time. Whenever he returned, she wanted to be ready with her carved knives. Therefore, she managed to drag herself to the kitchen each day to guzzle down whatever edibles her teeth could grab, hoping she would find enough strength to get up the stairs. But each day she tried, she failed, until Obigho returned.

Her heart lurched forward in her chest, attempting to flee, when she heard Obigho drive into the compound. She wondered what more monstrosities he had in store for her. But whatever it was, she was ready for it! The worst he could do to her was kill her. That was something she was quite prepared for! Her only pain was that she would have to take the breath of her unborn child with her if she died. That is, if the child had not already drawn their last breath.

As she heard Obigho's footsteps towards the door, she thought about all the insane things he could do to her, like tattoo his name across her face with a hot knife, gouge out her eyes and feed them to her to eat, hold her head over a burning furnace until her eyes dropped into the flames, or chop her bit by bit and feed her to the starving dogs outside. She trembled with fear as he turned the doorknob and flung the door wide open. She was afraid—terribly afraid—so afraid that she burst into a croaky laugh. Ireti laughed so hard that the thirty-room mansion shook as her laughter reverberated across the building! She thought about her friends, all of them despising their husbands as they gawked at hers, wishing they could take a walk in her shoes, wishing they could rip off their own skin to put on hers; she laughed even harder, bending over, rolling on the floor, and laughing!

Moments later, when she finally got a grip on herself, she looked up and found her husband kneeling before her. He seemed to have added two decades to his years since the last time she saw him; he looked very gaunt, too. The sight of him made her laugh even harder. How was it possible? How was it possible that she was the prisoner, but he looked every inch the part?

"Ireti, please, I beg you with all you hold dear, tell me where Abieyuwa is," he pleaded.

Really? To tell you where Abieyuwa is? That is all that is important to you? Really? Wrong button! Ireti thought.

"Ireti, please, for the sake of all we ever shared and for the love you once felt for me, please tell me where she is."

Wrong button, Ireti thought again as she started to weep.

As she wept, she started to drag the floor lamp again, struggling to go up the staircase for the umpteenth time. If she had any doubts in her mind about him dying, all that had flown out the window with his stupid pleas. She tried to go up the stairs again but could not move past the third step. Then she remembered. Damn it! Her captor was in a kneeling position.

"Unchain me now, you sick bastard!" she screamed.

"Will you tell me where our daughter is if I do?"

"Hell will freeze over first before I tell you where she is!" she heard herself say, instantly knowing it was the wrong response.

"Ireti, please pause for a minute to listen to the clock," he said to her.

She looked in the direction of the Maxwell Wall Clock, which had been presented to him when the prestigious Great Businessmen Association of Nigeria awarded him the Most Outstanding Personality of the Year a couple of years ago—it was some minutes past nine.

"Every second the clock tick-tocks away, life seeps out of my body."

"What exactly do you mean by that, Obigho?"

"I mean that I have been living on borrowed time these last couple of days. Every second I am not with Abieyuwa, I move closer to my grave. Please, do not let me die; I beg you!"

"Obigho, what exactly are you asking of me? Can you even listen to yourself? What are you asking of me, Obigho? I should bring you my daughter to defile for black magic so you can buy yourself some more time on earth. Is that what you're asking of me?" she asked him.

Obigho was taken aback momentarily but quickly found his voice. "Everything I ever did, I did for you... for us!"

"No! Obigho! No! Everything you ever did, you did for you! I never asked for this life you gave me. I was content being the wife of a bank manager."

"But you enjoyed everything I provided—"

"Yes! Yes! Yes! I did when I didn't know the cost. Now that I do, I know I do not need all these vain things you have provided. I do not, Obigho! I do not need all these rooms in this house. I sleep in only one corner of one of the rooms every single night."

"Forget your sanctimonious attitude for now. Couples do worse things to survive this cruel country."

"Emphasis on 'couples' Obigho! Emphasis on couples! You made the decision to literally eat our children alive all by yourself! I had no hand in it!"

"You had no hand in it? Really? Have you ever bothered to find out what kind of business I did to amass such incredible wealth in such a short time?"

"Imports and exports, you said."

"Importing what exactly and exporting what?" He got off his knees. "Look, I do not have the time for this. You see the clock over there; my spirit will leave my body when it chimes twelve at midnight. Doesn't that matter to you?"

"What's important to me is that you never lay your poisonous claws on my daughter, ever again!"

"Abieyuwa is but a small price to pay for all the comfort we have enjoyed over the—"

"Stop talking! Stop talking! You hideous monster! Stop talking! I know about the others, too! Obigho! What sort of monster are you? For every bloody bag of placenta you collected, you saw me fade away, yet—"

"I did—" he interrupted.

"Stop talking, I say! Stop talking before the pain I feel in the pit of my stomach gets to you before the clock does!"

So, the lovebirds sat watching, waiting, and paying close attention to every tick-tock of the clock.

When the clock chimed eleven, Obigho started to wheeze. Then he clutched at his chest and coughed incessantly. Ireti crawled to his side despite all the hatred she felt for him. She tried to, but could not stop the tears from pouring down her face in torrents. She bit her lower lip, cursing her luck and her ill fate. As she wept, she wondered if she was not making a grave mistake by not choosing her diabolical husband over her child. But Obigho chose this sad, solemn tune she could hear playing in the background now, and he should dance to it, she thought.

But how could she watch the love of her life suffer to his grave? She was about to give in when she remembered that the love of her life had watched her die every day as she buried child after child! Oh! He had flogged her mercilessly, not caring whether she would live or die. She remembered what she saw him do to Abieyuwa—her little girl's room illuminated by red candles as her husband heaved in and out of their daughter. Ireti recoiled, her movements as swift as a startled gazelle leaping from danger. She untangled her arms from around him and retreated, her resolve solidifying like the hardened bark of an ancient tree.

A few minutes before midnight, Obigho started to bleed from his mouth and nostrils, gasping for air.

"Ireti, Pl-e-a-se!" he gasped. Ireti felt moved to compassion again.

"Unchain me quickly! I need to call Tinuke!" she said to him.

He crawled up to the floor lamp, took out a small bunch of keys from his breast pocket, and unchained his wife. As soon as Ireti was set loose, she ran helter-skelter, searching for her phone. She ran up the stairs and searched their room frantically, but could not find it there. Then, she ran back down to the kitchen and searched everywhere but could not find the damn phone. Finally, she ran back to the living room and saw her husband ebbing away like dust exposed to the harsh wind before it dawned on her that she could just use his phone to make the call.

"Your phone! Your phone!" she shouted, rummaging through his pockets until she found his phone.

She dialled Tinuke's number, but her line was switched off! Then, she started calling all her friends, hoping someone would know where Tinuke was. Indeed, Tinuke was the right woman for the job, but now she wishes she had not picked her for it. She wept helplessly as she saw death easing slowly towards their door; she knew that no matter the barricade she put up, death, like water, would find a way to seep through.

Tick tock!

Tick tock!

Tick tock!

Tick tock!

Tick tock!

As soon as the clock chimed twelve, the chandelier dropped to the ground with a heavy thud, darkness enveloped the living room, and Obigho was gone!

She wept over him for a full hour before she got up, dried up her face, and went upstairs to take a cold shower as she prepared her story in her head. Yes, she knew she should have her story ready because, in Africa, men never die of natural causes or by their own making. It did not matter if the wife was a Stepford wife or an angel straight from Heaven; she would still be accused of killing her husband or looked upon with suspicion at his death. Therefore, it was crucial to tie all loose ends and prepare a good story for the in-laws and anyone else who cared for it.

Her 'perfect' husband was dead, and her daughter was free. She felt relief and sadness all at once.

Obigho deserved the death he got, she affirmed to herself. Nonetheless, she felt she owed him his reputation as a good and loving husband. Therefore, she locked away the true story behind his death in the deepest enclave of her heart and threw the key away. The cooked-up story was all she knew now and all she was willing to share. Her in-laws could, therefore, badger her all they want. They could dig up Obigho and arm him with more machetes and amulets if they liked. He died of natural causes. That was her story, and she was sticking to it, no matter the cost!

So, she endured four months of whispering and side talks whenever she went to the stream to get some water; four months of facing the senior wives of the family every morning, knowing how creative they were when it came to torturing a fellow woman in mourning; four months of finding comfort on a withered raffia mat and enduring the sonorous songs of mosquitoes; four months of waiting to see her children again; four months of thanksgiving for the soft jabs her belly received from time to time from the inside, despite all of the traumatic experiences they both had been through; four months during which Uncle Obe accidentally set the Maitama mansion on fire and everything burned to the ground. He had recounted that he was only lucky to get away with his life. She was not surprised; Obigho had told her everything they owned would turn to ashes as soon as his eyes closed. Fortunately, she had sold off the cars he bought her during the two-week period he was away, right after seeing him with their daughter, and stashed the money away in a new account she opened.

Every day for those four months, she received news of Obigho's wealth vanishing into thin air. After calling Tinuke to check on her children each evening, she would wait until the house was quiet to check her account balance. If there was a whirlwind sweeping away her late husband's wealth, she wanted to be able to look it in the eye and dare it to touch the money she had saved. She felt entitled to whatever money she had saved from her years of torture; she also wished she got a chance to move the money out of the safe like she intended, but Obigho never used the safe again after she set up cameras to watch him input the combination. She doubted Uncle Obe at first when he said he could not recover even a needle from the building, but she remembered Obigho's words. Whether Uncle Obe carted away the money or not, only time would tell.

Pa Ozua and the others determined there was no reason to detain her in the village any longer as soon as her belly started to show, especially after it was confirmed she was carrying their late son's son. They told her she could return to the city to manage her late husband's wealth, despite knowing there was absolutely nothing left to manage. They had fleeced her of all the money she had on her, but Ireti was not worried; she had the money in the bank, thankfully. She thought about the billion things she could do with all that money. She was excited that there was something to fall back on that could still somewhat give her the luxurious life she was accustomed to. What she feared the most was becoming like the chandelier in their living room, which once towered majestically over everyone, only to crash ferociously to the ground for ants to dance on. This fear crept up on her while she ate and while she slept, until she became so consumed by it that she could no longer breathe.

As soon as a date was set for her to leave the village and return to the city, she started caring less and less about who caught her spying on her account balance. She would check it as soon as she awoke, right before she had a meal, on her way to the bathroom, and before she slept at night. She kept checking and checking, so full of crippling fear, until she made up her mind to overcome her fear. What was she even thinking? How could she even think she would enjoy the money, knowing how it came? How would she be any different from her husband if she kept even one of the cursed coins?

On the eve of her departure from the village, she prepared her résumé under the moonlight, polished her shoes until they shone like polished mahogany, then selected a beautifully patterned Ankara dress, ready to embark on her journey back to Abuja. With determination burning in her heart, she vowed to start over from scratch and rebuild her life from the bottom up. If the funds she stashed away survived the hurricane sweeping away her late husband's fortune, she would give it all to the poor as a token of hope and a symbol of a new beginning. She planned to enrol Abieyuwa in a school designed for her needs and nurture her other children with gratitude and grace. Ireti knew the path ahead would be bumpy, but she was ready to embrace every twist and turn with the heart of a warrior.

Being with a Fat Girl

I am Samuel Onoja, and I love fat girls—not all kinds of fat girls, though; they have got to fit my *selection criteria.* To simplify things, I drafted a list on my seventeenth birthday, around the time my fascination with fat girls began—just a few days after my mother's best friend tore my heart to pieces.

"Sammy, we cannot continue this anymore—whatever it is we are doing." There was a long pause. "Your mother is my best friend, and you are like my son. I held you in my arms the day you were born. It is wrong to be with you, and I hate to think what your mother might do to me should she find out about our affair," she said, batting her long and full lashes.

Then, she paused and took a long, hard look at me, waiting for my reaction. I do not know what response she expected, but I simply told her to go back home and get some more sleep. Because, really! If it took her four years of what she usually called 'amazing sex' to figure out that our relationship was a bad idea, then perhaps she woke up on the wrong side of the bed. She simply needed more sleep, and her brain would reset itself. She insisted she was not joking and did not want to see me anywhere near her house anymore. Also, she would no longer come to mine, especially when my mother was not around, which was when she frequented our house the most since our affair began.

How was that even supposed to work? Her son and I are best friends; she is my mother's best friend, and her husband is my father's business partner. There was just no way our paths would not cross. So, what is she going to do? Just look the other way when we have family dinners, and pretend she did not enjoy my now X-marked penis more than she was enjoying whatever meal my mother served? How could I explain to Tim why I could no longer visit him at home? Breakups work better when both parties are not so complicatedly intertwined by life. She was older, so I expected that age would have made her privy to such knowledge.

"Bimbo, go back to bed!" I ordered. I was not joking either!

Well, neither was she.

The next day, I expected her to call and tell me the coast was clear and we could tumble in the hay as usual, but that never happened. Now, part of our memorandum of understanding was that I was never to call her residence, but I desperately needed to speak to her as I did not understand the strange pain in my heart that I somehow knew only she could make go away.

So, I called.

As soon as I heard the voice at the other end, I wanted to hiss and drop the phone, but how could I? What other reason would I have for calling the Adeolu Residence if not to speak with my best friend, Tim?

One week passed, and still, I had not even whiffed her perfume, let alone heard her scream, "Sammy! Oh! Sammy! Harder Sammy!

You rock my world, Sammy! Swee... sweee... sweeeeeet Sammy!" underneath my rock-hard body as I took her to the high heavens and back.

No word! No visit! Nothing! What would I do with the ring I bought to give her on my birthday night? What? It was the most expensive thing I ever bought. And it took a lot of careful planning and luck to raise the money.

First, I planned to steal the money from Mummy's purse on a perfect day when she had just returned from the market after making bulk purchases from Balogun Market.

Mummy usually loaded her bag with enough money to buy the entire market whenever we shopped. She would make me endure hellish trips with her, walking around the market until we nearly lost our legs to weariness while searching for the 'cheapest' purchases. I would carry her bag, and Mummy would dig into it to dole out cash, never recalling how much she spent in total or sometimes how much she even took to the market. If I stole from whatever she returned home with, there was no way in the world she would know her bag had had an unwelcome guest. But the market day never came. I wanted to shift attention to Daddy's briefcase, but he had recently changed the password.

That very stingy and selfish man! I thought. The poorest rich man I ever met!

He and Tim's dad made so much money, but not a penny ever made it home. It always went to booze and younger women, whom they could never keep up with. Those two were one-of-a-kind. It made me wonder—was Tim's dad so lousy in bed, forcing his wife to sleep with me, and was Mummy as dissatisfied as Tim's mum?

Wait a minute. Did Mummy have a small boy to service her, just as I did Tim's mum?

I shook the thought off. What Mummy did with herself was none of my business. My only concern was raising money to get my heartthrob a ring so that she can take me a little more seriously, and believe me when I say I am madly in love with her.

The first time I told her I loved her, she shook her head in pity and told me I did not know what love was. I was offended. I may be young, but everyone knows I am mentally and even physically older than my age, and I would prove it to her.

But where was I? Oh yes, the ring!

So, I often marvel at how the forces of life align sometimes to make a person's dreams come true. When it happens, it means that those things were meant to be. Why else would fate drag Uncle Omachi to our house just a week before my birthday?

"Ah! Birthday boy, how are you?" Uncle Omachi gasped.

Yes, Uncle Omachi gasps when he speaks. He is that fat. I suspect the fat moves up from his bulky stomach to block his throat when he speaks, making the words tumble like an evil revving engine. But that is not my problem. In fact, I pray that he eats and drinks himself to death so that I can inherit his wealth when he passes on, as I am the closest thing he has to an heir.

Uncle Omachi is from Daddy's side of the family; it is no wonder he is stingy, too. That unique ability to be tight-fisted must be in the blood. Anyway, Uncle Omachi miraculously offered to give me a birthday bash, mainly because I had just passed my university entrance exams. As a sharp boy, I told him not to worry about a party because I needed to save all I could for school and requested cash instead. My eyes popped when he brought out his purse from underneath his one-hundred-kilogramme arm and took out two wraps of crispy two-hundred-naira notes—like I said before, the forces aligned!

Early the next day, I rushed to the jewellery store and asked for the finest ring my money could buy. As I did, I rehearsed how I would propose to her and make her see that age—as they say—was only a number. I was going to make her the only woman in my world and make her see that Tim's dad was no good for her. Only for her to sleep on the wrong side of the bed and ruin it all!

After waiting for an eternity for her to call or visit, I decided that enough was enough. I would walk into the Adeolu residence and demand that she pack her things and elope with me to a place where we no longer needed to hide from anyone. I was heading for the door when the doorbell rang. I opened it, and it was a delivery boy. He handed me a parcel, which I signed for, and walked away. When I opened it, tears filled my eyes. In a small box was the necklace I got her for her fiftieth birthday, a symbol of our enduring love, which I had told her to wear daily. If she was returning it now, it only meant she was dead serious when she said it was over between us. If only she knew what I gave up getting her that necklace; if only she knew the sacrifices I made to buy her that precious gift... I wept.

I wept like the naïve little boy I was, believing that a woman like Bimbo could love someone like me.

That day was also my seventeenth birthday. I had nothing to be thankful for, so I stayed cheerless in my room all day, licking the wounds Bimbo had inflicted. It was also the day I resolved never to date any slim, confident, and beautiful woman ever again! I would get my pound of flesh one way or another. I took out my pen on the night of my birthday and made a list of my fat girls' selection criteria.

1. She must be fat, obviously!

2. She must have a not-so-bad-looking face—but only I must know this.

3. She must be of marriageable age and in dire need of a suitor—the more desperate, the better for me.

4. She must have a steady income.

5. She must be intelligent; let's face it: fat and dumb is a hell of a horrible combination.

6. She must be generous; the same reason as above applies.

7. She MUST possess little or no self-esteem—the sort you cannot sleep with if you do not turn off the lights.

8. Again, she must be ridiculously fat!

I memorised this list and burned the paper in the middle of the night. It was a sort of ritual for me. It felt like I was burning Bimbo's memory with it, as I had only one desire burning in my mind: REVENGE!

Shortly after the breakup, Daddy made a wrong business decision—probably because of the curses Mummy had been hurling at him for being irredeemably stingy and irresponsible—and the family business crumbled to the ground. From then on, Daddy and Mummy fought if the sun shone too bright and if the moon did not come out in full. The last straw that broke the donkey's back was when Mummy accused Daddy of stealing some money from her bag. Do not look at me. I swear, I did not do it.

Mummy packed her things and moved out of the house, leaving me and my three older sisters to choose sides. Mummy was more generous and loving, but I knew Daddy would turn the house into a brothel with whatever money he had left. Well, Mummy was too much of a 'Christian' for me, so a brothel was therefore a better option, as it was more in line with my mission. I decided to stick with the overtly annoying man.

As Daddy's business went down the sewage pipe, so did his relationship with Tim's dad. The man never showed up at our door again. He was apparently not just lousy in bed but a 'friend for food' too. Tim gained admission to a university in the UK, and distance somehow got in the way of our friendship. Having resumed the university myself, I was not around much any longer, so I never saw Bimbo again. Even though I have no idea what happened to her, I hope that she died! I sincerely hope that her beautiful skin was first riddled with leprous sores before she was finally crushed to death by a rickety truck by the roadside.

I met my first fat girl in my first year at the University of Jos. Lucy was her name. When I approached her desk to pay my school fees at the bank, I observed that she was smiling at me. I immediately remembered my list, made my mental checks, and by the very next day, I had her screaming my name on my hostel bunk.

Yeah, I am a charmer.

We moved our love tent to her apartment, which I only left if I had classes to attend or some other fat girl to chase.

Lucy was not, in my opinion, very generous, although the peanuts she threw at me, while expecting me to be highly grateful, were enough to pay my way through school. I would have been content to stick with her until at least the end of my second year, but her weight-loss strategy got in the way! Oh my, it involved a concerning amount of beans. Daily, a whole pot's worth, to be precise. Now, I would not normally judge someone's dietary choices, but this was bordering on a biohazard situation. I would have looked the other way; after all, she was not pouring all the beans into my stomach, but how could I? How could I when she would finish the pot of beans and nearly fling me out of the room with her forceful farts? I tell you, if one could fart out fat, Lucy would have become as skinny as a toothpick. But here I was, stuck with the massive weight of a forever-farting girl. I wanted to endure the farts until the forces aligned again and sent me shelter, a sheath for my rod, and some money for my pockets, but I was suffocating.

So, I decided to talk about it.

"Sweetheart," I started in the middle of the night as we lay in bed, her weight squeezing the life out of me as she lay 'cosily' in my arms.

"Yes, Honey," she cooed.

We had just finished making love, which I endured, but she enjoyed.

I cleared my throat. "Don't you think you've been overeating beans lately?" 'Lately' means the past year!

"You know, it's for my weight loss," she replied, a tinge of anger in her voice.

"Yes, I know beans help, but I don't think it's in the way you do it."

"How am I doing it? Ehn? Tell me. How?"

It was apparent she was already irritated. If only she knew how irritated I was, gasping for breath as I held her in my arms. I could not care less at this point.

"I think you overeat it!" I finally said.

"What's the meaning of that? Are you calling me a glutton?" she asked, lifting her concrete pillar of a body off my chest, thankfully.

I knew it was a trap, so I did not reply, though I desperately wanted to shout YES! YES! Yes, you are! Instead, I calmly switched to the main agenda.

"My love," I resumed, hoping to calm her down a bit. "Don't you think it is offensive to fart in my face?"

"Ehen? What is wrong with that? Are we not lovers?"

I did not think I heard her right. "It's okay to fart in my face because we are lovers?"

"Yes, nah. After all, we will be married as soon as you finish school."

I absolutely had no idea I had proposed.

"Once we do, are we not going to be farting in each other's faces? You should even be grateful I am farting now because the woman who farts in your face is the one who has nothing to hide."

Coming from a woman who never lets me see her naked, even when we make love? My jaw dropped, a sudden wave of anger coursed through my brain, and I felt a sudden urge to just strangle the ape right there and then. "Lucy, lovers or not, it is not acceptable for you to fart anyhow you like in my presence. Don't you have any shame?"

"Why are you calling me names over ordinary farts?"

Wait, hol' up! Did she just refer to those pit-latrine-smelly-farts as 'ordinary'? I wondered.

"First, you call me a glutton," she continued, "now, you call me shameless over common farts."

As she continued her lamentation, I did not know what came over me, but I suddenly did not care if I became homeless, eating from a dumpster, or pushing barrows to survive in school. "Yes, you are a glutton! You eat like a pig! You are fat, ugly, and shameless, and your farts smell like you have ten decomposing bodies swimming in your stomach!" I honestly do not know what came over me. I was usually the guy who concealed all of his demons behind a charming smile. I guess the farts really got to me. As soon as I said the words, I knew I would regret saying them, and I was right! Lucy got up quietly, brought down my suitcase, threw in some of my things she could find around, pushed the box out the door, and started to push my naked body out the door.

"It's two o'clock in the morning!" I cried out loud. "Where do you want me to go at this ungodly hour?"

She did not say a word; she just smiled eerily as she tossed me out and slammed the door shut in my face.

That night, I learned valuable lessons, the most vital of which was knowing the right time of day to pick a fight with a woman.

From one fat girl to the next, I was able to pay my way through school, as Mummy's boutique business died a few years after she left Daddy, and she was no longer able to support me. On the other hand, Daddy proved Mummy right: he was irredeemably irresponsible! Uncle Omachi refused to die, though layers and layers of fat had eaten through his arteries, so there was no inheritance for me. Fat girls saved my life! You may be wondering why fat girls, despite my obvious resentment for them. Well, low self-esteem is the answer.

I assumed that self-confidence was one of the reasons Bimbo messed me up, hence the desire for the plus-sized ladies. A fat girl who knows she is fat, hates that she is fat, has tried and failed at losing weight, and has given up on doing anything about her weight is easy prey for a guy like me who really just needs to survive. She may be the most incredible woman that ever walked the face of the earth, but she might never know this because people hardly ever focus on the things they have. They feed the lust for the things they lack, and when they try and fail at getting those things, they sink into depression and self-loathing. The fat girl, who already loathes her body, makes it easy to convince her of other areas she is not so spectacular at. And bingo! You have yourself a woman who is ready to bury a thousand bodies for you just to hear you say the words: 'I love you.'

I find these types of women easy to identify. They are the ones who hide every part of their body in oversized clothes, irrespective of how curvaceous their bodies are. They are the ones who forget to change their nail colour, wear makeup, or get the raggedy wigs off their heads. They have simply given up on their bodies. In my opinion, they already hate themselves; I only help them hate themselves better by making them love me. Call me a brute or any such name you so desire. But hey, life is a jungle; only the strong survive!

***

Over ten years later, I still haven't found a decent job. It feels like even God is folding His arms and staring at me because I graduated with an ordinary pass.

I keep saying it that a certificate is never a test of a person's worth. I hear Bill Gates is even a school dropout, as is our very own dear Tuface. Yet, they make a whole lot of money in their chosen paths. I believe I will hit the jackpot soon and finally move out of Daddy's godforsaken house someday.

I continued to date fat girls and always knew when to systematically pull out of the relationship just when they started to think we were headed down the aisle, leaving a lot of broken-hearted girls in my wake. Well, it was either their heads or mine. What could I have done? Life was neither sugarcane sweet nor *dogoyaro* bitter until I met Azuka.

Azuka was the only daughter of a renowned preacher in Lagos.

She was fat, ugly, had zero sense of fashion, and was a 'born-again Christian'.

How convenient!

We had dated for about a year, and I was about to take off when she called to say, "We need to talk."

Everyone knows that phrase never makes a good cup of coffee, so I suspected she wanted to break up with me, considering how harshly I had been treating her. But hey, come on, aside from Lucy—who, by the way, called to apologise the next day—no other fat girl ever had the guts to break up with me. So, I was a bit curious. I rushed to her Ikoyi apartment and knew at once from the look on her face that she had terrible news to share.

"Samuel, I missed my period," she said calmly.

"Oh! How can I help you find it?" I asked absent-mindedly.

"Don't be ridiculous, Samuel. What I mean is, I'm pregnant."

The bomb hit me hard! "What do you mean you're pregnant?"

"We fucked, Samuel. Remember? Then, I got pregnant."

'Fucked?' from a born-again Christian girl? I was surprised.

If this *bitch* thinks she can use her baby to tie me down, she had better think again! Earlier, I had anticipated something like this, so I started withdrawing sexual benefits and refusing to touch her months ago. When she whined and complained bitterly, I told her I had developed a medical condition that affected my performance. My urge for sex now only comes occasionally, like the sporadic rains of the dry season.

She had held my hands, prayed with me, and began her research to fix me up. Then she started to buy watermelons, dates, moringa leaves, and everything else known to boost libido. It is strange that she could find a cure for my disease but not for hers. I hissed silently. Me? A horse in the sheets to eat watermelon for libido? When my 'medical condition' eased, I gave her one last show to remind her who the real boss was, and now she claims she is pregnant? What nonsense!

"Hey lady, I used protection, so you had better go and find out who the father of that bastard is!"

"Condoms are only 98% safe. It's written on the pack. Besides, I somehow knew you would argue, so I kept this safe."

She reached for a small cellophane bag and brought out a used condom. I could not believe my eyes.

"See? The condom broke!" she said triumphantly.

I grabbed her by the throat. "You manipulative whore! I will kill you if you try to pin anything on me. You hear me? I don't care how many broken condoms you provide. The ape you are carrying isn't mine!" I flung her on the sofa and bolted for the door.

Stupid *bitch*! No wonder she had been cajoling me to meet her father, the pastor, so he would tie our nuptials. When that failed, she resorted to baby blackmail. Nonsense! Gone are the days when women forced men to marry them just because they stupidly got pregnant. These days, if you cannot flush your bastard down the drain, you should damn well take care of it yourself! Rubbish!

I expected her to make some trouble, so I prepared myself well! I was willing to swear by Ogun, Sango, Amadioha, or any other god to prove the bastard she carried was not mine! I waited weeks and months for my phone to ring with her number on the screen, but it never did.

***

Because life was too short, I quickly moved on to Amaka.

Oh, Amaka! She was the hottest fat girl I had ever met, and she was also the most confident and adventurous. She took me to bizarre places, where we went at each other like we were fighting for our lives. If I thought I was wild in the sack, Amaka was the true definition of WILD!

Oh! The things that girl could do to a man!

She made me sing la... la... la! It was unfortunate that I was not a rich man. It was quite unfortunate indeed, because if I had all the money in the world, I would have placed it all at her feet just to say THANK YOU! She made me feel nasty things—feelings I never thought possible, even in my wildest imagination!

I met her at a bar I frequented in Lekki. The moment our eyes met and she flashed me the most seductive smile, I was enchanted and started following her around like a lovestruck teenager. She would call in the middle of the night and say to meet her up behind the fence of a bank, and right there, we would have mind-boggling sex. We did it in several banks and restaurants, behind churches, in old warehouses, and in uncompleted buildings; we almost got caught doing it behind a mosque. We were weasels on rampage! She took me up, she brought me down, she turned me around, she turned me over, and she whisked me away!

Amaka literally set my soul on fire!

Ah! This was it for me! I made up my mind to quit all my *shit* and propose to her.

One night, Amaka called me to come and meet her somewhere. Because I anticipated our usual *sexdezvous*, I hurried to the location she gave. It was a dark, lonely road; I was a bit afraid but excited nonetheless. As I scanned the area to find a comfortable spot where we could have a royal rumble, she gave me her bag, said she needed to relieve herself, and asked me to wait for her.

If I had not been thinking with my *joystick*, I would have asked why she needed to go so far away from me to ease herself.

Before I could blink, sirens started blaring, and a police van pulled over. Several armed officers rushed towards me, and one hit me down with the butt of his gun before I could think of escaping. Next, I was taken to the police headquarters in Lagos, where I was beaten to a pulp as a welcome treat.

During my trial, I learned I was Kobosail, AKA The Dragon, AKA Bullet—a notorious criminal, more deadly than Anihnih of Edo State. According to them, I was responsible for most of the crimes perpetrated in Lagos and its environs, including several robberies of banks, restaurants, churches, and several business places. I was involved in vehicle theft; I had killed several policemen, and most recently, I had raped and murdered the daughter of a retired army general. Of course, I denied all the allegations, but sadly, my fingerprints were at all the crime scenes. There were even pictures of me leaving some of the scenes. No wonder Amaka insisted we wear masks during our sexcapades. She had designed the same mask that Kobosail wore during operations for me. The bag she gave me to hold had several packs of cocaine, two guns, and ammunition. That was more than enough for the police, who, by the way, were eager to please the influential personalities interested in the case, to send me to the gallows.

Amaka set me up, but I did not know why. How she distorted the CCTV footage from different locations and kept her fingerprints off the bag and everywhere else still beats me to this day.

I never saw her again until the day after my trial, where I was sentenced to life imprisonment and shipped off to Kirikiri Maximum

Prison. She came in the company of a gorgeous woman and a baby. My heart flew out of my chest as soon as I recognised her companion. It was Azuka! She seemed to have gained some confidence from Amaka, as she was clad in the most elegant red dress that accentuated every curve of her body. She wore her self-acceptance like a shimmering robe and embraced every curve and contour of her body with brazen pride. She exuded such dignity, grace, and poise as I had never seen since after my seventeenth birthday. I would not have recognised her without the familiar look of hate in her eyes. The little boy she held was my replica. I did not know what to say; I just stood and stared at her. Then I looked at the boy and went back to her again.

Apparently, she and Amaka came to gloat. Amaka, as I found out, was her evil cousin who was married to Kobosail. Azuka had run to her after I threatened to kill her, and Amaka had paid two kobo for the fight. She managed to pin all of Kobosail's crimes on me by giving me his identity.

Amaka said they came to tell me that they would tear my son apart bit by bit until there was nothing left of him. That was to be their final act of vengeance. I could not tell if they were bluffing or not, but something about the icy eyes of Azuka made me beg them desperately to please leave a little piece of me in the world because—come on, let's face it—this was no Prison Break, and I am no Scofield. With no big shot in my corner and no money in my pockets for a bribe, I knew only my corpse could walk out of these prison gates. Indeed, the poor should have no business making enemies. The little boy Azuka held in her arms may very well be the only child I might ever have. I pleaded endlessly for forgiveness, but their eyes bore no mercy until my time was up.

As I walked back to my cell, where I was sure my cellmate would batter my anus again, the great truth in William Congreve's words dawned on me, and I wondered how he could still be so right several centuries later.

"Heav'n has no rage like love to hatred turn'd,

nor Hell a fury, like a woman scorn'd."

A Place Without Heroes

"We all must understand that service is critical in our line of work," Jimoh Adegoke, the operations head of the Kugbo branch of Top Bank, advised his subordinates. "Exceptional service delivery is the fuel that drives our business. It is what distinguishes us from our competitors. You all know we offer the same products, but the quality of the service we render will make any customer choose us as their preferred bank. So, as we go to our various desks today, we must remember that the customer is king, the customer is always right, and the customer is the one who pays our salaries! He is the reason we are here! We must, therefore, ensure that we delight all the customers who walk up to us today. Today, we must all decide to bring on our A-game! We must all represent the bank's name in all we do today—Top Bank! Let us be top in all we do today, top in how we greet the customer with a smile, top in how we carry out our duties, and top in how we go the extra mile to delight and retain our customers!"

He felt proud of himself for the way he was able to go on and on extolling the bank and inspiring his people when he felt less than inspired, and indeed, he could not care less about the words he said himself. There was a time when he said those words and truly believed in them, but now he was angry about many things, particularly the fact that his wife could not even apologise for over-salting his breakfast for the millionth time that morning. What was so tricky about making scrambled eggs, for goodness' sake, that she just could never get it right? Here he was busting his ass off, literally working himself to the bone to provide for the home, yet he could not even get his wife to fix him breakfast without her emptying a whole jug of salt in a small bowl of eggs. He had advised her several times to use measuring spoons to put in the salt, for goodness' sake, but she just would not listen! She said she preferred to measure with her eyes and fingers just as her mother taught her, but her mother may have either taught her wrong, she had not paid enough attention, or the problem was with her eyes and fingers. The worst part was that each time he complained about the food being oversalted, she would accuse him of constantly complaining and being ungrateful instead of simply apologising. This morning, she had even had the nerve to tell him to fix his breakfasts himself going forward if all he could do was complain. He had perfect verbal punches to throw right back at her, but he was running late for work. So, he just simply told her how utterly useless she was!

"Very useless woman you are!" he yelled as he zoomed off in his car to make it to work on time.

She was useless—utterly useless! He worked from seven in the morning until seven in the evening. Sometimes, he closed later. He never ate lunch at home, and on most days, since having a pot belly was something he could not tolerate, he settled for a cup of tea for dinner after dealing with the traffic to get home late. Breakfast, therefore, meant everything to him, and it was all he ever asked of his wife. Yet, she managed to mess it up for him every single time!

Another thing that upset him that morning was the academic performance of his first son, Fisayo. His wife showed him the report card the boy had brought home from school the previous day. Fisayo was eleven but always came in third from the rear in his class in all his academic years. They had already changed his school six times, and now the boy attended one of the most expensive private schools in the area, yet he still could not acquire an expensive brain. What the hell was wrong with that boy? Where the heck did he get such a fish brain from? Certainly not from him! In his day, he always came at the top of his class. He was a high-flyer. How could he be so cursed with a dullard for a son?

While preparing for work each morning, he stared at the boy with distaste. The boy would snuggle under the thick covers, with his head left open, for the air conditioner to chill his pap of a brain even when he should be awake already, getting ready for school. He could not blame him at all. If the boy had been exposed to garri and kuli-kuli for breakfast, lunch, and dinner like his father at his age, instead of the bread and butter he constantly stuffed his mouth with like a fool, he probably would have been brighter in class. Who knows? Maybe the boy's mother's oversalted meals caused his predicament. Thankfully, the other three children took after him. He mused.

The third reason why Oga Jimoh, as his subordinates called him, was upset that morning was his car, a 2006 Honda Accord. Driving to work angrily that morning, he noticed thick smoke trailing him. It was apparent that the car's engine needed to be replaced. Indeed, the car needed to be replaced. But how could he afford to change his car when he had not received a salary bump in over twelve years, despite how hard he worked? This was the biggest reason Oga Jimoh did not feel inspired that morning. How could his organisation leave him stunted for over twelve years without any explanation? When he got the job twelve years ago, he was promised promotion every two years if he worked hard enough and received excellent appraisals. Twelve years later, he had kept his own end of the bargain, but his employers had fallen short every damn time. They kept increasing his responsibilities and job titles without any corresponding promotion or pay increase. The organisation broke his heart several times when it seemed like his name was being missed during each promotion exercise, only to be suddenly remembered when there was a new task or more enormous responsibilities to be undertaken. Several times, he had felt so frustrated with the work that he wanted to just *cut out*, but *cut out* to where?

To where, exactly?

He lived in a country where you needed to know somebody who knows somebody who knows somebody before you could get a job, no matter how qualified you are for it. The new government had promised him CHANGE, but the change it brought could not give him the pleasure of even changing his cursed car. It brought nothing but untold hardship everywhere he turned. How, then, could he aspire to change his job when he was only fortunate to still have the one he currently has in the first place? Since the current government took over about three years ago, over two thousand of his colleagues have lost their jobs as the bank had to cut down on staff costs to survive the economic crunch. Those who remained had to do more work to make up for the manpower lost, yet they were expected to be wonder workers, maintaining the same service level as when they had full staff strength. And because the employers knew they had nowhere else to go, skipping names during promotion and getting away with any ill-treatment meted out to the staff was possible. So, when Oga Jimoh motivated his staff to put in their best efforts on the job that morning, he said it mechanically because it was what he knew his employers expected him to say. Moreover, he had no other ideas on how to keep providing bread and butter for his block-headed son and fresh eggs for his wife to over-salt. So, he said the words with as much passion as he could muster.

"Before we end this meeting, I will ask each of you what specific challenges you face on the job that could affect service delivery. Let us start with customer service. Angela?" Oga Jimoh called, shifting his gaze towards Angela Chinenye Okoro, the Head of Customer Service, who joined the branch nearly three years ago after a redeployment from a Lagos branch following her marriage to a man who lives in Abuja.

When asked what her job challenge was, she wanted to say that she needed to be home to care for her sick son. In the middle of the night, her domestic help eloped with their security man, leaving her to deal with all the household problems alone. The primary concern was how to care for her sick baby, who had been suffering from malaria for about two days. She felt guilty when she woke the ten-month-old up at five that morning to prepare him for the emergency creche that she was thankfully able to arrange when she woke up to find the domestic help's bed empty. She was also exhausted, having been up all night due to her son's persistent coughing. But how could she possibly explain all this to her boss?

"The major challenge we have is ATM disputes," she told her boss instead. "With the new platform deployed, transactions take longer to resolve, which has left customers angry and dissatisfied."

"Well, there is really nothing we can do about that at the branch level. We'll continue to mount pressure on the head office team for quick resolution, but you must manage the customers well. You know there's a way you can tell someone to go to hell, and they'll look forward to the trip. Please manage the customers," Oga Jimoh finished with Angela and moved on to her support staff, John Tom Nelson.

"Sir, we require additional staff at the customer service desk. The two of us are unable to manage all the customer complaints alone. We receive over two hundred requests daily, and at this rate, we cannot meet the turnaround time."

"Hmmm... you'll need to work smarter because we're even lucky to have two staff at the customer service desk. Some bigger branches have just one customer service officer. Recruitment is not the bank's present mood—layoff is. So, if you love your job and want to keep it, you must find a way to make it work despite the challenges."

Oga Jimoh knew he was too hard on John, but what the heck? It was what his own superiors would have told him if he had opened his mouth to spit out such nonsense.

Next, he turned to Bello Mustapha Musa, the cash officer. Like most others, Bello was interested in something other than this early Monday morning meeting. It was just the seventeenth of the month, yet he was dead broke already. Off the top of his head, he was owing twelve people real money as he was recently a victim of a Ponzi scheme. If only he had followed his instincts and not joined. However, he needed quick cash to marry his third wife, and since nearly everyone he knew was doing it and making lots of money, too, he had decided to give it a try.

First, he put in fifty thousand naira and received a hundred and ten thousand back in just two weeks! Then, he reckoned that if he put in all his savings, totalling one million, six hundred thousand naira, he would make double the amount and some change in another two weeks. So, he cleared out his accounts and took a significant risk for a substantial gain, only to have a considerable loss just one week later. With his wedding coming up by the weekend, he would have probably committed suicide to save face if not for the many people and places he was able to get loans from. It did not help that he was a cash officer so severely in need of cash.

"Sir, the major challenge we've been facing is that recently, a good portion of the cash received from the cash centre has been coming with many shortages. Biodun has been processing most of the cash from the cash centre for ATM load and has discovered several short packets. Sometimes, I even make up the cash with my own money. If we could talk to the cash team about being more careful when processing the money—"

"We'll see what we can do about that," Oga Jimoh added. "In the interim, you must ensure you run all the money you receive from the cash centre early enough to mitigate against losses."

Next, he turned to Biodun Taiwo Olajide, Teller 1 for the branch, also known as the Yoruba Demon. Biodun was not only interested in the boring meeting ending but also eager for business to close for the day. Yesterday, while his wife and children were in church, he had spoken with Janet, the girl he had been tracking for over a month, and they had agreed to meet today after work. He was so grateful he had feigned a running stomach when his wife tried to pressure him into attending church service with the family. How would he have struck this deal with Janet if he had gone to church? During the office meeting, he sat behind Angela, counting on her voluptuous frame to shield him as he chatted on WhatsApp with his best friend, Kehinde. Kehinde was his partner-in-crime. Being a single guy, Kehinde always gave up his apartment to Biodun to host his vast array of girls, but he required him to give him ample notice to take down his own picture frames and put his friend's own up before he showed up with the girl. Biodun was trying to give Kehinde this notice before he left for work himself.

"Biodun, I'm waiting for your feedback," Oga Jimoh said.

Biodun looked up, lost.

"I asked, what challenges are you currently experiencing on the job?"

'We don't close early enough, sir,' he wanted to say. "No challenge, boss!" he heard himself say instead.

"Over to you, Ibraheem," Oga Jimoh announced.

Ibraheem Musa Mohammed was Teller 2. His wife just had a bouncing baby boy, and he could not wait to get home to discuss the naming ceremony with her.

"Sir, I need new stamps. The ones I have now are worn out and do not appear clearly when I use them on transaction slips," he said quietly.

"Remind me later in the day so I can contact the store for new ones," Oga Jimoh said before turning to Mariam Aisha Bagama, Teller 3.

Teller 3 was eager for the meeting to end. She had exams that afternoon and was completely unprepared. She had thought that the weekend would be enough to cover the semester's work, but menstrual cramps had made her life miserable at the worst possible time, so she could not meet up. Now, she hoped the meeting would end quickly so she could glance at her course materials before sitting for the exam at two o'clock. To be better prepared for her exams, she requested that part of her annual leave be used to cover the exam duration, but her supervisor rejected her request, citing the bank's current staffing situation. According to her supervisor, no one was available to relieve her, and the other three tellers would struggle to handle the workload without her. He had, however, permitted her to take a few hours off to go write the exams and return to work daily until she was done. It would have been an okay arrangement, except for days like this, when her time off work was insufficient to prepare for the paper. She barely heard what Oga Jimoh said throughout the meeting, as she was too anxious to pay any attention to anything he had to say. She was quite sick and tired of being an ordinary contract staffer with no hope of ever being elevated to anything else. That was all her Higher National Diploma could fetch her—lots of work with a slave's pay! If she wanted something better, she needed a B.Sc., which she was striving to get, if only she could pass today's paper and every subsequent one.

"Mariam, do you have any challenges on the job?" Oga Jimoh asked her directly.

"No, sir," she replied.

Oga Jimoh shifted his gaze to Teller 4, who was staring at his wristwatch.

Obinna Ebuka Nwamadi was expecting the laptop seller at about ten that morning, and he could not wait! He had been able to get a good deal from the seller. He would be given any laptop of his choice and allowed to pay in instalments over four months. Since his earnings could not afford him one outright, this arrangement felt like a godsend, and he could not wait to show off his new baby.

“Obinna? Any challenge?” Oga Jimoh asked.

“None whatsoever!” Obinna replied.

“Okay, we're running out of time. So, for the cleaners and the security team, the heads of the unit can speak for their teams. Zainab Yakubu, you'll speak on behalf of the cleaners since your head of department called in sick.”

She's not sick at all! Zainab almost yelled, but she could not rat out her madam like that.

Her madam, Omotayo Clara Botu, travelled to Kaduna over the weekend to cater for a wedding and was yet to return. Anytime she was contracted to cook for an event, she would call in sick and make the other cleaners work until they nearly dropped. Cleaning the branch was a difficult enough task when there were three of them. Leaving only two of them to do the job was just cruel. What made Zainab angry the most was that she had never brought them even toothpicks from any of the events she catered for, let alone shared some of the extra bucks she made with them.

“Sir, I think someone has been stealing some of the detergents we clean with. The same quantity that used to last us a month cannot even reach us two weeks now.”

“Really? Someone is stealing detergent in a place like this?” Oga Jimoh was alarmed. “Where do you usually keep the detergent?” he quizzed.

"At the old store upstairs."

"No, move it downstairs into the new store where the CCTV cameras can monitor the place. I want to use the thief as a scapegoat," he said, with emphasis on scapegoat.

Tanko Aliu, the other cleaner present, was grateful he was not asked to contribute because he was not in the mood at all. A week ago, he found out he had Hepatitis B at a free Hepatitis B screening organised by the community where he lived. Initially, he refused to participate, but his wife convinced him it was for their own good. Now, look at him, unsure if he still has a future. What would happen to his five children now that he and his wife had the virus if the local medicine of mixed herbs he was taking for treatment did not work? He would have preferred to go to a real hospital for treatment, but when he went into the government hospital for inquiries, the cost of even running the various tests for himself alone was more than his six months' salary. If only he had health insurance. Sadly, cleaners and all ad-hoc staff did not enjoy such luxuries. The stupid community people could organise free screenings but not free treatments, thereby just handing them their death certificates and walking away.

"Do the marketers have anything to add? Kolade, you can speak for the group," Oga Jimoh said.

"I think our major problem is the car issue. For over a month now, the only car in the branch has not been good enough to take anyone out for marketing. The branch driver was also among those sacked two weeks ago, meaning there's no plan to fix the car anytime soon. How do we bring in business when we're not mobile?" Kolade Abel Adebayo lamented on behalf of the marketing team.

"The car requires major repairs. The approval process is a little more tedious now, so you all will have to be patient, though it is not an excuse not to bring in business. Once the car's fixed, getting another driver shouldn't be a problem."

Kolade wanted to protest, but Oga Jimoh gave him a dismissive look and turned to the security personnel.

"James, any challenge?"

"All correct, boss!" James Ubong, the branch's chief security officer, spoke for his team.

"If there is no other matter arising, we should adjourn this meeting so we can proceed to give our customers a great time today. We must all remember to be at our very best so there will be no bad report about the branch awaiting the branch manager, who is currently on leave. Have a nice day, everyone."

Just as everyone started to disperse, James quickly approached Oga Jimoh. "Ehen, sir, Iliyasu gave me this letter to give you last week, but I forgot." He dipped into his back pocket and fetched a brown envelope rolled up like a cigarette. He tried to smooth it out, but Oga Jimoh impatiently took it from him. He looked at it and saw that it was addressed to the branch manager.

"Where is it from?"

"Iliyasu said one woman brought it upper weekend, sir, but he gave it to me to give you last week."

Iliyasu Abdullahi quickly ran off the scene before he was asked any direct questions about how the letter came to be. Oga Jimoh tossed the letter in his drawer, believing it was a random letter from a complaining customer. He prepared for vault activities before ushering in the customers already queued up at the gate outside, and only remembered to revisit the letter some minutes past eleven o'clock.

Angela was concerned about her baby all day but still offered her customers plastic smiles. She wished she could steal some minutes to check up on the boy, but she kept receiving customer after customer and could not get away.

Mariam tried to read in between customers, but after overpaying one by ten thousand naira, which she knew she would be forced to pay at the end of the day, she was compelled to drop her books and just concentrate on work with her heart pounding in her chest, worried she was inadequately prepared for her exam.

Biodun truly treated his customers nicely. With a new *babe* waiting to be devoured by him that evening, absolutely nothing could dampen his mood. He felt rather proud of himself. He knew he was not a very good-looking guy; he knew he even leaned more towards being ugly and did not have a lot of money either, yet the girls followed him like butterflies to nectar. His midsection was his selling point; he knew it, and the girls knew it—end of discussion! Customer after customer, he kept stealing glances at the wall clock in the banking hall, subconsciously waiting to hear the closing bell.

Kolade had a prospective customer to see that morning, but there was no way he would use his money to transport himself to the customer's office! He shrugged his shoulders, "If they like, they should fix the car; if they don't like, they should not fix it. None of my bloody business!" he cursed. He, too, was upset. He felt cheated by the organisation, too. For some years, he had not been paid any extra commission on his deposits, which made him furious. Every month, he was given a new financial target, and every month, he exceeded the target but got no extra commission on the enormous deposits he had been bringing in despite the bank's promises. It made him even angrier that other marketers at his level had smaller targets. The explanation always given to him was that each month he had to do better than the previous, and being that he started off on a far better note than his counterparts, his target would keep growing because 'the reward for hard work is more hard work', he was told.

He felt used and underappreciated since all his hard work did not translate to a fatter bank account. Now, the bank could not even provide him with a working car to get around. Today, he was going nowhere! If not getting the business he was supposed to get that morning would sink the bank, then by all means, let it sink!

Obinna was getting rather impatient and upset. It was past ten, yet the laptop seller had yet to show up. He snuck out of his workstation to call him several times, but he just kept telling him he was on his way.

"On your way from where? Maiduguri?" he shouted into the phone. "I wonder why Africans never stick to time!" he fumed.

Zainab and Tanko were having a dispute over the duty roster. Tanko did not understand why she expected him, as a man, to clean the women's toilet. And why was he the one who had to go to the food vendor to get breakfast for Oga Jimoh? Zainab argued that with Omotayo away, she had the authority to assign him any task she wanted.

Oga Jimoh could no longer placate his hunger pangs. If he had known that he would not have time to think of his stomach once the customers trooped in, he would have sent one of the cleaners to get him Indomie and fried eggs from the Mallam across the road before the doors were opened. Now, Indomie would not just cut it for him. He needed something heavy that would pass for breakfast and lunch until he got home for dinner. Today, he craved real food all through—no noodles, no tea. Hopefully, his wife will not cook him salt tonight. As he retrieved money from his drawer for Tanko to purchase pounded yam and white soup, he noticed the letter again. He tossed it on his table and instructed Tanko on what to buy.

"Oga, pounded yam fit never ready by this time o," Tanko told him.

"I really want to eat pounded yam today. It's been a long time since I've had some. Check if it's ready; if not, wait for them to finish making it, and bring it to me very hot and fresh," he instructed.

As soon as Tanko left for the food vendor's shop, Oga Jimoh picked up the brown envelope, tore it open, brought out the letter, and froze when he got to the body of the letter.

"Ahn ahn! Ahn ahn!" he kept saying. "Where's James? Somebody, get me James very quickly!" Ordinarily, he would have picked up the intercom to call James, to maintain a sense of decorum, but now was not the time! John, who sat nearest to him, ran off quickly to get James, sensing the urgency in his boss' voice. As soon as James approached him, the boss shouted, "Where the hell did you say this letter came from?"

"Oga, it's Iliyasu who gave it to me o!"

"When did he give it to you again?"

"Last week, sir."

"Since last week? Since last week, and you're just bringing it to me?"

James could not understand why his boss was so furious at him for forgetting to bring the letter to him early enough. But I had explained myself earlier, he wondered.

"Where did Iliyasu get it from, and where is he right now?"

"He said a woman gave it to him the *upper* weekend."

"Upper weekend? You mean two weekends ago? So Iliyasu received this letter two weekends ago but didn't give it to you until last week, and you are stupidly only bringing it now? Where the hell is Iliyasu?" he cursed, seemingly unaware of his surroundings.

"He is on night shift, sir. He left immediately after the meeting."

"Get him back here at once!" Oga Jimoh barked as he quickly ran to a secluded area of the office to call his boss, the Regional Head, regarding the letter's content. As the phone rang, he kept gazing at the letter.

Dear Sir,

AN OFFER TO ROB YOUR BANK

We are delighted to inform you that we will be coming to collect all the cash you have been keeping safe for us next week.

We shall come very prepared. You should, too.

Thank you in advance for your cooperation.

Warmest regards.

When his boss picked up the call, he read the letter to him.

"Okay. When did you receive the letter?" his boss asked.

"I got it this morning, but the security man said it was brought two weekends ago."

"Two weekends ago, and you only got it this morning? How are you people working in that branch of yours? Issue that security man a query and copy his staff file. Let him explain the reason for such negligence. But scan the letter immediately and send it to the bank's chief security officer. Let him handle logistics to beef up security at the branch."

"Okay, sir."

"Hold on a minute! Did you not say in the letter that they would visit next week?"

"Yes, sir," answered Oga Jimoh.

"And you got the letter two weekends ago?"

"Yes, sir."

"Doesn't that mean they should have visited last week? The letter might be a hoax. We received several similar letters at my previous bank, but they were either empty threats or silly pranks."

"I don't think so, sir. This letter is dated the ninth, when I believe it was delivered. It was a Sunday, meaning it's this week, they must mean."

"Well, today is Monday. Most bank robberies occur on Fridays, so we have ample time to beef up security, but still scan and send the document immediately!" his boss told him.

Oga Jimoh was unsure where his boss got the statistics from or when he became a robbery expert, but he was relieved that they may not be in danger today. He returned to his desk and sent the document as instructed, but no matter how hard he tried, he could not get his mind off the letter. So, he called his boss again.

"Sir, I have a terrible feeling about this security threat. Don't you think we should email HR to inform them we need to close the branch this week?"

"Are you being serious right now? You mean we should send the customers away and lose revenue for an entire week because of some silly letter you got? What is wrong with you? You're making me doubt the decision to allow you to head that branch. Can you imagine? We should close a branch for an entire week and let our competitors scoop up our customers? Do you have any idea how much the bank would lose if we closed our doors for even a day?"

"I apologise, sir. It's just that—"

"My friend, please get back to work and remain vigilant. Tell the police officers on guard to be on alert. Don't spread panic; tell your staff to look out for and report suspicious movements. By the way, have you sent the email to the CSO?"

"Yes, I have, sir. I copied you," responded Oga Jimoh.

"And has he replied?"

"No, he hasn't, sir."

His boss quickly scanned through his inbox. "He hasn't? A mail that was sent over thirty minutes ago?"

"No, he hasn't, sir," confirmed Oga Jimoh.

"Put a call through to him and keep me posted."

"Yes, sir."

Obinna could not take his eyes off his boss from the moment he called for someone to fetch James. He watched him go to a corner to make the first call. Although he could not hear what was being said, he could tell something was wrong. His eyes followed him again as he made the second call and several others that followed. He observed him whispering to the cash officer, then moving on to do the same with the Head of Customer Service, before heading outside to speak with the police and security officers. Obinna grew increasingly convinced that something was definitely amiss. He immediately asked his supervisor, the cash officer, what was going on and what the boss had said. But he just casually replied, "There's no problem," and advised him to return to his desk to attend to the customers. Obinna returned to his desk but kept a close watch on

Oga Jimoh, distracting himself from his anxious wait for the laptop seller.

The cash officer heard what the boss whispered in his ear loud and clear. He even saw the fear in his boss's eyes, but he was not afraid. Somehow, he felt calm about the situation. He thought about discussing the boss's fear with Obinna but decided it was better to let sleeping dogs lie. He did not believe they were in any apparent danger, so there was no need to cause unnecessary panic. Despite his confidence that no harm would come to them, the thought crossed his mind to go and mop up cash from his tellers' cubicles to at least maintain the bank's counter limit, but he was too distracted by his wedding plans and how to make some extra bucks before the wedding day.

As soon as Angela heard about the threat, her heart started to skip beats, and she began to regret the decision to come to work that day. Maybe her domestic staff of over two years eloping with their security man and leaving her alone to care for her child was a sign—a bad omen. Perhaps the sick child was another sign that she should not have come to work that day. She should have just called in sick, but she feared getting into trouble. Since she returned from maternity leave some months ago, she has always felt that her colleagues looked at her differently, as if they expected her productivity level to drop. Every day since then, she has been in competition, not just with herself but with all her male colleagues. Now, look where her overzealousness has landed her.

Oga Jimoh instructed the police and security officers to be alert, scanning and monitoring the environment for unusual and suspicious movements due to the threat letter received. Following the advice from the bank's chief security officer during a phone call, he requested the on-duty police officers to call for reinforcements. They were making the call when he went back into the building. As soon as he got in, he looked in Angela's direction and saw that her face had become white and pale with worry. He knew she was terrified to death but could not afford to have one of his strongest hands buckle under now, so he went to her and whispered in her ears to stay calm as security had been beefed up. Besides, it could just be a silly prank and there is nothing to worry about. She gave him a shy smile, heaved a sigh of relief, and continued rapping away at her keyboard.

At exactly half past noon, Oga Jimoh received a call from the Head of Operations of Top Bank, Nyanyan Branch, with the news that Golden Rift Bank, the bank behind them, had just been robbed and almost all the staff killed, while the ones lucky enough to survive sustained severe injuries. Oga Jimoh shared details of the unusual letter he had received that morning with him.

"Ah! That means you guys need to vacate the premises o because it may just be from the same guys who just left our area now. Those guys are on a rampage!" he warned.

Oga Jimoh quickly cut the call to call the regional head again to inform him of the new development.

"I don't think there's anything to worry about," the regional head dismissed. "It is even possible they mixed up the address and sent that letter to your branch in error—"

"But sir, I think we should take the advice of Amos and just close the branch until—"

"That is unacceptable! Does it make sense to you to close a branch at the East Pole just because one other got robbed at the West Pole?"

"But the atmosphere is tense s—"

"We simply can't afford to shut down a branch just because of how you feel about the atmosphere! Anyway, I'll speak to HR and get back to you shortly."

Walking back to his desk, Mariam approached him to get permission to go write her exams.

"Please feel free to," he said to her, relieved that he had one less person to worry about.

In fact, what was he even thinking? Why was he even paying attention to the regional head, who was swivelling in his chair as he dished out instructions from the city centre? He was the CEO of his own branch, and if his guts told him to move his staff out and shut down the branch, he would do just that. He knew he would face the consequences of his actions tomorrow, but today, he intends for himself and his team to stay safe.

Immediately, he instructed Angela and John to tidy up their desks for the day. He was about to walk to Bello to tell him he and his team should do the same when they all heard a deafening sound—gunshots that sent all the birds of the sky scampering and flying to safety. Through the window, Oga Jimoh and the others watched in horror as Mariam fell to the ground at the gate. As she fell, so did the police officers and security men on guard outside the building.

The banking hall was in chaos, with staff and customers calling upon the god or gods they worshipped. A customer in front of Biodun, who had just withdrawn a reasonable sum in dollars, quickly tossed the cash over the counter, disclaiming the notes.

Zainab was cleaning the toilets since that idiot Tanko refused to return from the food vendor when she heard the sound and the accompanying chaos. She wanted to rush out to listen to what it was all about but started hearing some customers screaming.

"Wayo Allah na! Wayo Allah na! Robbers oooo! Wayo Allaaaaaaaaaaaaah!"

Quickly, she locked the door of the restroom she was in and sat on the toilet seat, praying and sweating profusely!

The moment Angela heard the gunshots, her first thought was of her son; it was nearly his closing time, and he might wait for her in vain. Amid the chaos, she quickly picked up her phone and, with trembling hands, typed a message to her husband.

Robbers. Die. Ebuka. Pick.

The robbers moved to the mantrap door leading into the building and started to spray it with bullets. Thankfully, it was bulletproof. Those who had big hearts watched as the men sprayed on, hoping that the doors stood their ground—a formidable stronghold to shield them from their attackers. Only Oga Jimoh soon realised that the robbers were not spraying the doors—they were spraying the walls around them!

"We need to hide! We need to hide!" he told his team.

Several customers flew under tables. Some ran into the toilets until there was no more room to accommodate any of them. They tried to open one of the toilets, but it would not budge. Zainab alone sat in that one, stiff with fear.

"The safest place is the vault, sir!" Bello screamed over the sound of the gunshots.

"The vault, everybody!" Oga Jimoh shouted, and they all scurried there.

Upon running into the vault, they faced a significant problem: how to lock the place from within. The strongroom had a gate and a massive security door. They could lock the gate from within, but that alone wouldn't stop them from getting killed. Only the gigantic security door could shield them from the robbers, but unfortunately, it could only be locked by throwing the combination from without.

"Someone has to make the ultimate sacrifice for us all. As for me, my wife just had a baby," Ibraheem said to the group.

"Me, I am pregnant!" Angela said without batting an eyelid to shield the lie. There was no way she was going to die for anyone.

"My children are still very young, and my wife is unemployed," Biodun said. Then, an idea struck him, and he ran back into the banking hall.

"Me, I haven't even married, let alone have children. I cannot afford to die today," John said.

"So, who can afford to die? Is it me that will stay behind to lock the door when my wedding is just this weekend?!" Bello shouted angrily.

"But you have two wives and five children already. We don't even have one yet," Obinna accused Bello.

"So, because I have two wives and five children, that means I should die for all of you?"

"ZAN CHI UBAN KUUUUUUUUUUUUUUUUU!" They suddenly heard one of the robbers shout.

His voice sounded like rumbling thunder. The next sound they heard helped the pack make up their minds, and quickly too! The robbers sprayed around the doors until their apparent leader, a man with a large scar across his face and a red piece of cloth wrapped around his head, gave a chant to signal them to move away from the door. Then he tossed dynamite at the door. Just one blast, and there was enough room for a hoard of cattle to troop in through.

The leader led some of them into the hall. Some others stood guard outside the building; some more stood outside the gate; and a few more kept the van they came in warm and ready for exit.

"ZAN CHI UBAN KUUUUUUUUUUUUUUUUUU!" The leader, with eyes that seemed to be shooting fireballs, crouched and shouted again, signalling his boys to shoot anyone in sight.

Biodun was still stuffing in his pockets the dollar bills the last customer he attended to flung at him when the force with which the building tore open threw him into a corner. He was dazed for a moment but quickly regained full consciousness. He wanted to crawl under his table, but he knew that that would be unsafe because the first place the robbers would visit would be the teller area, where the money is. He had to get out of there fast if he wanted to live. Counting on the high marble counter to shield him, he started to crawl towards the vault as the robbers sprayed the place, killing everyone in sight. What he did not see coming was that one of the men would, at that very moment, leap on the counter. Five gunshots later, he was flat on the ground, dollar bills sticking out of his pockets.

Some gunmen blew the CCTV recorder into tiny pieces, while others loaded money into the large bags they came in with, passing them on to others who moved the cash into the van outside, while others scanned the entire building to still anything that moved. They went to the toilets first. There were three toilets: one marked female, one marked male, and the third marked staff only. They tried to open the first, but it did not open, so they moved to the second. They tried to open it. It wasn't locked, but it seemed something or someone was blocking the door from within, so they forced it open and rained bullets on everyone they met there. The discovery made them furious. They returned to the first door and tried to kick it open, but it wouldn't cave in, so they just repainted it with bullets and were about to move to the third door when someone shouted, "Upstairs! Upstairs!" and the men raced up the stairs. Zainab was behind the third door, terrified out of her mind!

Kolade was wetting his pants in a cabinet upstairs. He sniffed back the mucus that resulted from his stifled cry. He wished he had gone out like he had intended that morning. He really wished! As soon as he heard the first rounds of gunshots, being a sharp Lagos boy, he did not need a soothsayer to tell him what was about to happen. He thought about joining the others downstairs, but he had yet to make up his mind when the blast went off. He and the four other marketers quickly found hiding places and prayed that their heads remained intact on their shoulders.

Osmond Chibuke, a contract marketer, was not very lucky. He was hiding behind a shelf, but his legs were sticking out, so his legs cost him his head. If only his employers had not renewed his contract last month, as they had first threatened, he would have been home, probably trying again to make his wife of over three years conceive for the first time.

Inside the vault, Obinna could no longer help his curiosity.

"What is the meaning of 'zan chi uban ku'?" he asked Bello, a Hausa man among them.

"It literally means I will eat your father, as in, I will deal with all of you," he replied.

The place was airless and would have been pitch black with the vault door locked, but thankfully, John had his phone in his pocket when he ran in. They used the phone's flashlight to illuminate the area. The one thing Angela wished she had on her now was her inhaler. The longer they stayed in, the more difficult it was for her to breathe.

Outside the vault, Oga Jimoh quickly texted the head of operations at the nearest branch. His heart pounded fast and loud, like war drums. His entire body trembled like palm fronds in a storm. He was terrified of what was coming, but what could he do? If it were a typical robbery, he would have just had his team surrender the cash—the money was insured, after all—but this was no ordinary robbery. The robbers seemed intent on wiping them all out, as if on a revenge mission.

Revenge for what? That was what baffled Oga Jimoh. Who else was to be the sacrificial lamb than he, who was their leader? Besides, he felt responsible. They would have all been safe in their homes if he had trusted his gut. He had risked all their lives, and now he had to pay the ultimate price for it.

Both his phones started to ring, interrupting his thoughts. His boss was on one line, his wife on the other. He was too upset to speak with his boss and too sad to speak with his wife. He wanted to ignore them both, but as soon as the robbers blasted the door that led to the anti-vault where he was, he knew he had to hear his wife's voice one last time. He wanted her to know he was no longer angry with her and did not mean the mean things he had said that morning, so he picked up the call and put it on speaker. His wife was sobbing hysterically.

"Jimoh, one of your colleagues just called me now to tell me that you want to die for your colleagues. Please, in the name of all you hold dear, don't do it! Please, for the sake of our children—"

"You don't get it. Either one of us dies to protect the others, or we all die!"

"Ehen, but why must it be you? Why must it be you, Jimoh? Please don't be a hero! Please!" She started to sob again, but before he could utter any words of comfort to her, the face of death stood right before him. There was something dark and dreary about the way Death chewed on his tobacco. Perhaps it was his red, yet dark, hollow eyes, the large scar across his face, the way the red rag hung about his head, the black necklace with the skull pendant around his neck, or the overall darkness of his countenance, but only DEATH could have been a suitable name for him from the moment he was born.

"Ka na jin Hausa?" Death asked Oga Jimoh.

"Kadan kadan," he replied.

Kadan kadan would not be enough to pass on his message, so he switched to English.

"I and my guys need to get into that vault, and you're in our way!"

What surprised Oga Jimoh the most was how fluently he spoke English. He even spoke the language with a foreign accent. His polished English was in sharp contrast with his appearance.

"Open the damn door NOW!" the thunder was back in his voice.

"Jimoh, open the stupid door!" his wife ordered from the other end of the line. "Please, don't throw your life away for an ungrateful bank that hasn't appreciated all your efforts all these years."

"I am not doing this for the bank. I am doing it for my colleagues."

"Your colleagues? Do they love you? Do they care about you? No! They don't love you, and they do not care about you. If they did, you wouldn't be standing at death's door while they cosy up inside."

"But I am their leader—"

"And so? In this country, have you ever heard of a leader dying for his subjects? Here, the led are made to die daily in droves for their leaders to live. What do you think will happen to me and the children if you throw your life away? Heroes are never celebrated, Jimoh. Over here, heroes are fools. Please think about… think about our children," she wept.

"It is too late now, Fola. If I open, I die; if I don't, I die," he told his wife sadly, and the woman broke down in uncontrollable tears.

"Open the door, and I might just spare your life," Death said to Oga Jimoh.

Oga Jimoh wanted to believe him, but it was a gamble. Could Death be trusted? What if he complied and they all still died? What would have been the essence of holding on in the first place? Everything would have come down to nothing. But then what if he opened the door, and they just took the money and took no other lives with them? It was all a gamble. There he was, facing the most hideous man he had ever seen, and his wife weeping at the other end. What was he to do?

"Lokachin da yan sanda su ka bamu ya kusan ka re!" one of the men standing behind Death warned.

"Dan Allah, mu tafi, mu tafi!" Death's men started to chant.

Oga Jimoh did not understand the first part, where they said they had exceeded the time the police had allotted them, but he knew 'mu tafi' meant 'let us go' in Hausa. So, instead of opening the door as he had decided moments ago, he stuck it out since the men were already in a hurry to leave.

The walls of the vault were in shock! They wondered what was happening, each wall whispering to the other why the people before them had hearts that could pound so loud. Usually, they kept watch over ever gentle, quiet notes, with occasional interference by people whose hearts never beat quite as loud. Today was different. Today, people did not just pop in and pop out. Today, they stayed with the notes; they stayed with them! The walls observed silently as the people gathered around Bello, waiting for him to translate the next Hausa word to drop in from the outside, realising that their lives might likely depend on it. Together, they huddled, their hearts pounding fiercely in unison, as they listened to their boss debate whether they should live or die. Suddenly, one of them could not bear it any longer. She collapsed to the ground, writhing and thrashing, unable to breathe.

The walls felt sorry for her, but they could do nothing to help. Thankfully, Obinna took the initiative to strip her naked. It seemed to help a bit because the thrashing reduced. The walls could not look; they shut their eyes out of embarrassment. Obinna was not. He had always wanted to see what the most senior female in the branch looked like under her fine suits but never quite got the chance. He quickly flung her suit to a corner of the room and ripped her camisole apart. He was about to go for her bra when the others stopped him.

"Move away from her so she gets as much air as possible," John advised. He then put her in an upright position and encouraged her to take long, deep breaths.

The walls listened with curiosity as the hearts beat even louder, a part afraid of the danger lurking outside the door and the other fearful for the woman who might die in their midst if she did not get her inhaler soonest.

"ZAN CHI UBAN KUUUUUUUUUUUUUUUUUU!" they suddenly heard from the outside, followed by gunshots and a loud, piercing cry! Tanko repeatedly tried calling Oga Jimoh, but his line was busy. He wanted to explain that he had waited over an hour for the pounded yam, which was not ready because the food vendor ran out of yams and had to send her daughter to the market. He wanted to inform Oga Jimoh of this and perhaps ask if he should return to the bank, but he remembered the man's instructions.

'I really want to eat pounded yam today. It's been a long time since I've had some. Check if it's ready; if not, wait for them to finish making it, and bring it to me very hot and fresh,' flashed through

Tanko's mind.

It meant he was not to return to the office without the pounded yam. So, he waited. The food vendor kept calling her daughter, but the girl kept complaining about hold-ups and returned nearly two hours later. Tanko waited patiently for them to finish making the food and was relieved when the vendor brought it neatly packed in a plastic bag about forty-five minutes after the girl's return.

As he hurried back to the branch, his mind wandered off to Zainab and how she had become a snake basking in the sun and relishing her moment of glory—just because Omotayo was absent for a single day. He hissed; he did not blame her at all. If they had not left Bauchi for the capital city, she probably would have been one of his wives—maybe the fourth—waiting her turn to be made love to and kneeling to serve his meals, or even waiting on her knees until he was done eating so she could take the dishes to the kitchen to wash up for his next meal.

But now, they both worked as cleaners in a bank, and she felt she could flap her feathers to spread her bath water in his face. He hissed again and was still fuming when he walked into the traffic that had built up to the road leading up to their bank building. He asked a few passersby what could be causing the unusual traffic. As soon as he heard about the robbery, a strange fear gripped his heart. He did not know why, but he started to run like a lunatic all the way to the building, the food running with him.

By the time he reached the building, the robbers were gone; the police had come, and piles and piles of bodies were being brought out to be conveyed to the mortuary by the hospital van. One of the bodies caused Tanko to lose his grip on the plastic bag containing Oga Jimoh's food.

It was Oga Jimoh's!

The food splattered, further contributing to the chaos of the already messy place.

The regional head arrived to oversee the reconciliation of heads and cash. Zainab Yakubu survived but had to be forcibly removed from the toilet seat, as the fear of death had frozen her onto it. Iliyasu Aliyu also survived; working the night shift had its benefits. However, he walked around with his heart in his mouth, anticipating the inevitable. Upon learning of the tragedy at the bank while he was absent, he knew it was only a matter of time before the bank and the police turned their searchlight in his direction. They would discover that he was away from his duty post on the day the letter was delivered.

In truth, he had only temporarily left his post to be with Amina, the Indomie seller's first daughter. Along with the police on guard and the other security man on duty, they had called the Indomie seller that Sunday afternoon to request plates of noodles, and the man had sent Amina to deliver the food. The policeman and the other security man were to go in first for lunch while he kept watch of the premises until they were finished. He fully intended to wait for their return before moving an inch, but Amina winked at him as she left the premises. Knowing exactly what she was suggesting, he quickly followed her to an old shack in an uncultivated plot beside the bank. If only he had known that five minutes of pleasure could cause so much disaster! When he returned, the letter was lying on the ground in the compound. He never saw the person who brought it in, but when asked, he claimed it was some woman. Now, everyone would expect him to be able to identify that woman. There was no way the bank would not come for his head—no way at all!

One security guard survived by hiding in the toilet attached to the security post. Although someone had left it unflushed and the water supply was cut off, he figured a bullet would kill him faster than the terrible smell from the toilet bowl. So, he hid behind the door, holding his breath. Sadly, three other security guards were not so fortunate. They perished, along with Mariam, all departing this world within moments of each other.

The branch manager chose the best time to be on vacation, unlike Mariam Aisha Bagama, who worried all day about her exams when she should have been worrying about her head.

John Tom Nelson survived; he told anyone who cared to listen that he was now eternally indebted to Oga Jimoh and could not stop thanking his maker that the man did not listen to his knife of a wife, who spewed terrible advice from the ugliness in her stomach. Omotayo Clara Botu's lie had saved her, while the cabinet, which Kolade Abel Adebayo always thought was insignificant, gave him the pleasure of living another day. Who would have thought a day would come when he would owe his life to it?

James Ubong lived; he slipped out of the building to the Indomie seller's shop across the road immediately after he was informed of the security threat. He knew when the robbers came, and he watched them leave, but the fact that he was the branch's chief security officer did not mean he should die for the peanuts he was paid monthly.

Angela Chinenye Okoro narrowly survived. Fortunately, Oga Jimoh had given the vault door combination to the operations head of the nearest branch, who was on standby to release them once the robbers left. He arrived just in time before Angela slipped away. As for Ibraheem Musa Mohammed, he still had his head on his shoulders and felt immense relief knowing he could return to his wife and newborn baby at the end of the day. Ironically, in a few months, it would be extremely difficult to remember that Oga Jimoh left behind a wife and children.

The dollar bills Biodun Taiwo Olajide had stuffed in his pockets were recovered, but the bank refused to cover his burial expenses due to his 'abominable' act. His date for that evening waited in vain and only heard of his death a week later. Three marketers made it out alive; thankfully, they had better hide-and-seek skills than marketing skills. Osmond Chibuke died, but the war between his legs and his head was one that would never end. Like John, Obinna Ebuka Nwamadi survived and was grateful to Oga Jimoh but harboured resentment towards the man's wife. At the beginning of the day, leaving the office with his brand-new laptop was the most important thing in the world, but after the horrific events of the day, he was thrilled to be leaving with his head.

The laptop seller was found dead at the gate. He greeted Mariam at the gate just before he dropped to the floor, with his laptops lying broken beside him as he bled to death. Bello Mustapha Musa also survived; he felt immense relief to be alive, but that relief would soon turn to uncertainty.

Tanko Aliyu would remain eternally grateful to Oga Jimoh for wanting pounded yam so desperately that morning. He could never have imagined that a man as healthy as Oga Jimoh would leave this world before him, whose body was being ravaged by the hepatitis B virus. He still did not know how to heal his body, but he was thrilled to be able to breathe even for one more day.

It was at the moment that the bullets pierced his heart that Oga Jimoh remembered he had not eaten anything all day. He had imagined his death at times before this day, but it had never crossed his mind that he would die on an empty stomach despite his lifelong hard work. As blood spurted from his mouth and his spirit began to fade, his thoughts turned to his wife and the harsh words he had spoken to her that morning. He regretted never having the chance to tell her he did not mean any of them.

The three police officers on duty lost their lives, betrayed by their own colleagues who promised reinforcements but delayed until their bodies were cold. Ten customers managed to survive: two by feigning death and eight by using others as shields in the restroom. Thirty-two customers perished: ordinary individuals who merely wished to conduct banking transactions and return home to their loved ones. They were mothers, fathers, sisters, brothers—somebody's somebody, all now gone with the wind.

After the head count, the bodies were removed amidst tears, gnashing of the teeth, and screams that should have been enough to awaken the dead. Everyone sympathised with Oga Jimoh's wife, including those who viewed her as an evil woman for prioritising her husband's safety over his colleagues'.

The regional head then oversaw the cash balancing, meticulously managing the debits and credits and tracking what went out and what came in. Like a war commander, he issued instructions with precision and ensured that everyone continued to perform their best to balance the books despite the tears in their eyes and the fear in their hearts. If only top management could have witnessed his dedication then, they would have been so proud! What troubled him deeply, though, was how the robbers managed to leave with such a significant amount of cash if they did not have access to the vault. The only reason he could think of was that the cash officer did not adhere to the bank's counter-limit policy. So, that morning, when Bello woke up with thoughts of how to raise more money for his wedding on his mind, little did he know the day would end with him spending an unpaid vacation in the police cell. His wedding day would find him still swimming in a black pool full of snakes and sharks, with his identity card retrieved by the bank and an investigation into his involvement in the robbery in full swing.

Just before they were forced to shut down the bank at midnight, an angry rain came like a white witch to clean up the mess made during the day. She first washed clean the limp flag that bore the inscription: "Top Bank! Where You'd Rather Bank" before moving on to the flower beds. Then, she scrubbed the streets and floors clean. She paused momentarily to assess her work. Unsatisfied with the results, she took a mighty sweep with the help of a ferocious wind until the roof of the building was flung to a corner—the vault remained the safest place.

She continued to scrub everything and everyone in the building until they were all forced out, giving Angela the chance to finally be reunited with her son and husband. Thankfully, he understood the distress message she had sent him. He picked up their son from the crèche after work and tried to get the police to rescue his wife, but nothing he said made them increase their speed until they were truly ready.

The rain wept in torrents as Oga Jimoh's wife wept. She wished she could have changed so many things if only she could turn back the hands of time.

"He should have listened to me... he should have listened to me," the wife kept muttering to herself as her tears soaked her blouse.

She was the proverbial adult who could see while sitting down what a child could not see, even from a rooftop. She knew how the story would end, even from the beginning. His colleagues would spare her late husband a minute of their lives the next working day. For a while, she would receive condolence messages, many of which would come with promises of love and care for those the hero left behind—promises she knew would lie in the grave alongside the dead. She was not a seer, but the next couple of months revealed how absolutely correct she was.

The rain fell, stopped, fell again and again, and slowly, the memory of her late husband's heroic deeds was washed away too. Only she and her children would bear the scars forever.

The Weeds

Kofoworola was so nervous that she could barely steady her hands. So, she resolved to cook and clean as she always did whenever such overwhelming feelings arose. She brought out the vegetables she had bought on her way home from the adire fabric shop, which she managed with her husband, and started chopping them as if hypnotised. The fried rice she planned for the next day's meal was ready in no time.

After cooking the fried rice, she tiptoed into the living room to check on her husband for what felt like the millionth time since she had returned home earlier that evening. He was still rooted to his spot, glued to his favourite chair, facing the TV screen. His legs were stretched out, with one placed on the other in front of him; his palms were on either side of his chest; and his glassy eyes were fixed on the blank television screen where he usually watched the network news while she made dinner.

When she got home that evening, the first thing she noticed was that the front door was ajar. Her husband was not one to leave a door unlocked, at least not since that night twenty-three years ago when he forgot to lock the back door after going out to turn on the generator, and robbers had attacked them, leaving with the day's sales they had planned to deposit in the bank the next morning. Since then, he has become obsessed with locking doors. Something must be terribly wrong if he does not care about the door now. When she walked in and found her husband in that position, her heart sank, and she knew that sleep would elude their home that night.

The first time she saw him in that mood, she was alarmed. She tried to talk to him, but he stared at her blankly, like a spirit detached from its earthly vessel. Then she drew closer, looked into his eyes, and saw that he was not even blinking. At the time, they had only been married for five months—the five most amazing months of her life! But five months were not enough to know all about a person. Except for when he forbade her from working elsewhere aside from the adire shop he owned, and that one night when he returned home drunk. He could easily pass for the most amazing husband.

Amazing, until he started playing dead.

It was the first time, so she assumed that the spirit of death had either snatched him or was about to. She was frantically dialling the pastor's number after calling their family doctor on the phone when he suddenly let out a deep grunt and motioned for her to drop the phone and return to the bedroom. He stayed that way for two whole days. It was on the night of the second day when he had somewhat overcome the demons that had overpowered him, that he made her sit next to him on the edge of their matrimonial bed in the dead of night and quietly asked her, "Why did you smile back at Baba Kola?"

"Huh?" she asked, bewildered.

"Do you now need hearing aids? I said, why did you smile back at my friend two days ago when he visited?"

"But he's your friend... that's why. I was only being polite."

"Polite? Polite? You call that being polite? You know that he feels a certain hunger in his groin whenever he sets his eyes on you, yet you smile back at him? Or do you feel that same hunger when you look at him, too?"

"No, no! God forbid that I ever feel that way towards another man!"

"Oh! So, you knew what I was talking about all along, eh?"

"I am very sorry. It will never happen again," she apologised, expecting the words to work like magic as they usually do whenever she upsets him—but not this time! It took the intervention of family members before peace returned to their home.

The second time he slipped into such a state was during the sunless days when everything she tasted felt like raw bitterleaf. It was during the turbulent days that she wished she had never married so she would not have to bear some of the heavy blows life dealt her simply because she was wife to a man whose mother had a tongue that could cut through stone and whose mouth spat the venom of a cobra each time she spoke. Those were the gloomy days when, according to her mother-in-law, she was yet to be 'tested and proven'. As far as her mother-in-law was concerned, her marriage was planted on sinking sands, and she was hellbent on making sure the sands swallowed it completely.

When she knew that her son, Akinlade, had travelled out of town, she arrived one afternoon in a minivan with four hefty men and a young woman, who was to become her son's new bride. She charged into the compound like a tornado, stormed into the living room, and ordered the men to throw 'the cock and her belongings' out of her son's house. Kofoworola was too shocked to even argue.

Everyone knows that a woman marries a man and his mother in Africa, so she simply could not protest. She quickly picked up a few of her things and left in the van to go to her sister's place downtown.

A furious Akinlade arrived at his sister-in-law's door three nights later, demanding that his wife return to their matrimonial home with him immediately! As soon as they got home and he started to help his wife settle in, she gently held his hand in hers.

"Akin, maybe you shouldn't be so upset with your mother. I may be a barren woman, after all. Perhaps I am the cursed fig tree that can never bear fruit. You should listen to her and accept the wife she brought you so we can hear the cry of a baby in this house."

Akinlade yanked his wife's hand away from his as if she were holding a scorpion in it. "Don't you ever speak to me of another woman again! If you are tired of being my wife, simply say so, but never tell me to marry another."

"But, Akin, it's been five years already, and still, my womb feels as hard as a rock. It's like there's no soil for anything to grow."

"Five years isn't fifty. I can wait five decades to carry a child born by you, Kofo."

She looked into his eyes, knew he meant every word, and heaved a deep sigh of relief. But her husband did not sleep in their bed that night. She woke up in the middle of the night to find him 'in the zone', as she started calling it. Getting him back took two torturous days of extensive cooking and cleaning. But this would be only after her mother-in-law sent emissaries from Oshogbo to come and apologise to her son and his wife for sticking her nose where it did not belong.

The third and fourth times it happened, she started to look for patterns and possible reasons why he entered the zone so she could avoid future occurrences. She noted that the third time it happened was after he lost some money to the robbers who visited them, and the fourth was when he found out his most trusted salesman had been stealing from him. Before the discovery, he believed that he had angered some evil spirit, and they were after his business to bring it to its knees. When he discovered the evil spirit was Dele, his most trusted salesman of over thirteen years, Akinlade was inconsolable. Kofoworola, therefore, concluded that only two things put her husband in the zone: his woman and his money.

After her discovery, she took over the management of the business funds and ensured they never lost a kobo again. At home, she tried to be the best wife possible. This was made even easier when, a few years down the line, she gave birth to their only son, Jide. Her womb only produced that lone seed, but it was a good seed—a male seed, a beautiful and exceptionally brilliant male seed—and a seed potent enough to cut off the venomous tongue of her mother-in-law and pluck out the leering eyes of friends worse than foes. It was a seed so meaningful that her husband never revisited the zone—until now.

Kofoworola's mind raced through the events of the day repeatedly, from when they exchanged greetings in the kitchen as she prepared breakfast to when they drove through the narrow streets of Ado-Ekiti to the adire shop. At about ten minutes past ten that morning, he told her that he needed to return to the house to pick up some documents for the family lawyer. Before she could protest, he drove off in the old truck that served as the family ride and the delivery van for their business.

She remembered that Akinlade never returned to the adire shop. She had tried to call him, but his phone was switched off, only for her to close for the day and return home to find him drowning in depression. What happened when he got home? She knew they had not lost any money, and she had done nothing wrong to upset the man. If she was not the problem and money was not the problem, it only meant there was a new demon in town.

Kofoworola tiptoed to the living room again to check on him, but he had not stirred since the last time she left him. She wanted to engage him by asking what happened or whether she had done anything wrong, but experience had taught her that those questions never yielded fruit until her husband was ready to come out of his shell. So she returned to the kitchen to show off some more culinary skills. She cooked until her fridge was full of food that could last them a lifetime. As she cooked, she prayed her husband would take pity on her and snap out of his madness. It had worked well the last two times. However, this time, he did not seem to care if she worked herself to death.

'He cannot see you toiling to death in the kitchen. Take the drama to the living room, where his unseeing eyes cannot pretend not to see you,' she said to herself.

So, she went into the living room and started to clean. First, she removed the cobwebs and dusted the chairs. Next, she wiped the electronic appliances; she cleaned the items as if her very existence depended on how brightly they shone. Afterwards, she put her frail and ageing knees to the ground and scrubbed the Persian centre rug until it screamed for mercy. She cleaned the glass table on top of the Persian rug until it shone brighter than the sun. Her hands were bleeding, and her body was buckling under the weight of all the work, but her eyes remained steady and fiery. If her husband could put up a show, so could she!

Moments after she finished scrubbing the tiles in the living room as if she intended to serve the food she cooked all evening on them, she fell to the ground, panting and exhausted to the bone. Then she gave her husband a scornful look.

'You win, you wicked, horrible man!' she raged silently in her mind.

She stretched to the side stool beside the sofa to reach her phone, hoping to call her son to come and talk some sense into his father. Perhaps he would succeed where she had failed. Both men adored each other. Akinlade was exceptionally proud of Jide, especially since he returned from the US two months ago after completing a course in economics at Princeton University. On the day of Jide's arrival, Akinlade ensured the boy received a hero's welcome. He also showed him around and grinned from molar to molar as he bragged about how his son was the true son of his father. If anyone could make the old man snap out of his depression, it was definitely Jide. But where was he? It was a little past eight in the evening now, and Jide had yet to return home. He never got home later than five on most evenings, so she added that to her worries.

"Please, have you heard from Ji—?" she tried to ask.

He did not let the words finish falling off her tongue. "Don't you ever mention that name in this house ever again!" he growled. "That boy is dead! Dead! DEAD!" he barked, returning to his trance.

Oh! So, it was Jide who plunged you into the abyss of depression? What did he do wrong? Kofoworola wondered.

She had never witnessed them in any sort of fight; she often teased that he should have married his son just because of how much he adored the boy.

"Why? What has he done?" she asked, but the question hit a brick wall.

She sat on the floor, her legs sprawled out in exhaustion, and her head and arms spread on the sofa in confusion, until she drifted off to sleep.

At nine that evening, the squeaking of the door jolted her awake, and she lifted her weary waist off the floor, waiting for the intruder to show their face. Looking up, she noticed her husband had not as much as moved a muscle. But as soon as the light hit the intruder's face, Akinlade jumped up, pointing a gun at him that he must have hidden behind his back the entire time. Kofoworola impulsively threw herself in front of the muzzle while the intruder stood defiantly, his hands hanging loosely beside him as if to say, 'What the heck! Shoot me, please!'

"Woman, get out of my way. Let me kill this bastard who parades himself as my son!"

The words 'my son' made bile build up in his mouth, so he quickly spat out the bitter taste on the tiles his wife had only earlier mopped clean with her blood.

"Kill me, Father. I am sick and tired of your holier-than-thou attitude! Shoot me dead, please!" Jide spat back.

Akinlade cocked his gun, ready to fire, but in the same instant, Kofoworola turned to the boy and smacked him hard across the face. That seemed to appease the old man a little, and he fell back into his chair, his chest heaving as if he had just climbed Mount Kilimanjaro and wrestled evil spirits while at it.

"How dare you talk to your father like that?" she asked. The boy stood subdued. Kofoworola fell on her knees before her husband. "Please put his sins on me. Whatever it is he has done, I am to blame. Kill me, please, but please don't break my only eye," she pleaded, tears streaming down her cheeks.

"Yes, exactly! You are to blame! It is all your fault!" Akinlade fumed, visibly frothing in the mouth.

"What are you talking about?" she asked, calmly wiping her tears with the ear of the wrapper around her waist.

"It was you who ruined our son. I told you to keep him in a school in the country, but you insisted that your son must study in America." He flew up again, the heavy weight of the air around him pushing his wife to the ground.

"See him now! Your American baby! See him all spoiled and rotten, dripping with maggots and pus! Woman, behold your rotten American son!"

"He is now my son? Just my son? Did we not both agree that we wanted the best education for our only baby boy?"

"Yes, best! Best! But Nigeria's best, not America's best!"

"Best? In Nigeria?"

"Yes, best in Nigeria!"

"With all the endless strike actions and the quality of education relentlessly tumbling down the hill? How can that ever be called the best?"

"Well, look what your America did to our son! Look at him now—a basket full of rotten tomatoes! I told you America has absolutely nothing good to offer, but you said all your friends have children studying abroad. Now look, our son is one huge maggot dump!"

As her husband stabbed her with his words, the woman's eyes rested on the inscription on his shirt: I LOVE AMERICA!

It was one of the shirts Jide had gotten him when he visited two years ago. Akinlade had worn the shirt very proudly to the adire shop every day until its black colour started to slowly turn white, and she intervened by begging him not to wear the shirt out again but only wear it indoors. How could he stand there now and say that nothing good could come out of America when almost everything they owned came from there? Was it not he who always insisted that Jide order and ship even the tiniest things needed for the house from there? Maybe Jide was right after all; Akinlade did have a holier-than-thou attitude. But she could not say that. She could never side with her son over her husband, no matter how wrong he was.

"But I don't understand. Only yesterday morning, you were still bragging about having the youngest business guru in town. What changed?"

"Everything! Everything has changed! The scales that blinded my eyes to the truth have gone with yesterday."

"What truth? Huh, Akinlade? That he isn't your son?" Kofoworola could no longer hide her bile.

"Ask him! Ask him what I caught him doing this morning!"

"What? What did he do that could be so wrong that you want him to pay with his life?"

Akinlade jumped to Jide's side, still wielding his gun. "Tell your mother what you did this morning!"

The boy stood stiffly in defiance, but his quivering lips betrayed his fear.

"I say, tell your mother what you did, or have witches chewed off your tongue?" He turned to his wife. "His mouth is too heavy to say the words." Then he gave a brief, mirthless laugh and continued, "Maybe there is still hope for him if he still feels shame."

"I am not ashamed of anything! I did not do anything wro—" He did not finish saying the words because his father pushed them right back in with the butt of his gun.

"Oh my God! You have killed him! You have killed him, Akin!" Kofoworola rushed to her son's side on the floor, screaming. She left the boy and grabbed her husband by the neckline of his shirt.

"Please, you have to kill me too!"

Just then, Jide groaned in pain, and his mother raced to his side and placed his head on her thighs, weeping as she did.

"What did he ever do to you? I have told you that your evil temper will ruin our family one of these days. Why do you want to kill our son?"

"He is not my son! He could never be my son!"

"Why? Why? Why, Akinlade?!"

"Because no son of mine would ever be caught pants down with the neighbour's son!" he yelled.

"Ehn?" Kofoworola shrieked, letting go of her son's head as if she had just noticed that he had leprosy. Jide winced as she stood up and very slowly walked towards her husband. "Akinlade, what exactly do you mean by pants down and the neighbour's son?"

"Please, which of the words do you find confusing so I can explain in detail? I said I caught your son drilling vigorously into the anus of Wale, our neighbour's son!"

"What?!" Kofoworola squealed.

"Yes! He was in a deep tango with Wale. He was screwing viscously into Wale. He was buried deep inside Wale, swimming in his shitwater. His groin was super glued to Wale's behind as he rode him like a demented horse on our matrimonial bed!"

"Stop! Stop! Stop!" Kofoworola screamed, holding her ears closed with both hands.

"Why are you screaming and blocking your ears? Open them wide, please. Let me explain what your precious American son has been up to in very clear terms. He was wiping Wale's anus with his baton, firing down with reckless abandon, and slamming into him. Wham! Bam! Wham! Bam! Wham! Bam! Wham! Wait, let me show you." He started to take off his clothes.

"Stop! Stop! Stop! He is still my son; stop! Pleeeease!" Kofoworola cried, collapsing to the ground and breaking down in uncontrollable anguish.

Her husband, weakened by her tears, rushed to her side and held her in his arms.

"You see now, my dear, we prayed to God for a son, but he sent us a faulty package. That is why I say you should let me return this damaged product back to the sender quietly."

"No, Akin! He is still our son! We shall do no such thing!"

"Your son, not mine! This monster can never be my son. Let us return him to wherever he came from before he ruins us completely. Can't you see? He wants to drag our name through the mud—a name we toiled so hard to build."

"But he's our son! How can we murder our own son, our only baby boy?"

"It isn't murder when you kill a monster! Any man who rams into another man is a monster!"

"I cannot believe you. I cannot believe I have lived with you this entire time and never seen this side of you."

"Well," he shrugged, "my eyes have seen the back of my head. What do you expect?"

"He is still our son. Take a look at him lying there. Swear you feel no love for him despite everything," she said to her husband, staring at their son.

"No, you take a good look at him. Picture him slamming all of himself into Wale. A boy! Both of them groaning like overfed calves and pouring their dirty shitwater and smelly sweat on our matrimonial sheets. Swear that you don't feel so repulsed by the sight of him that you'd rush into the kitchen, grab your pestle, and grind his head into the ground like you grind yam in a mortar. Swear!"

At that moment, Kofoworola looked at her son and felt something she had never felt for him—disgust! She felt nauseated by the mere sight of him and rushed to the bathroom to empty her guts in the toilet bowl while her husband followed to help her clean up.

"You see what I mean? Let us put him out before the morning light. We brought him into this world; we can also take him out of it, no problem!"

"No! I can never kill my own son!" she yelled.

"Why don't you face it? Your son is already dead; America killed him. What we have lying in there now is a pig draped in a shirt and jeans—a monster!"

"Yes, he did something horrible, but how do we snuff life out of our own baby while that useless Wale who defiled him still breathes clean air?"

"What are you suggesting? Are you saying we kill them both? It would be our little contribution to making the world a better place."

"No! I mean, it would be unfair to punish our own son while Wale lives without the consequences of his actions. If anything, he is to blame for coming in here to ruin our son."

"What makes you think the reverse isn't the case? I strongly believe it is your son who has brought this obscenity into our lives, not Wale, who is even too dumb to spell his own name, let alone comprehend how to fix his hose in a man's hole. From what I saw, your son defiled Wale. I say we pluck out Jide and Wale off the surface of the earth before they ruin us all! Let us remove the weeds from amongst us before they take over the entire farmland."

"Your mouth says things your hands cannot do. You know how I know this? Do you remember the night of Jide's birth? You were so excited about the birth of our child that you insisted you wanted to be in the room the moment he arrived. But you could not stay. You said the room was full of blood, and you passed out. It's how I know your mouth is braver than your heart. Akin, killing our son isn't the solution. If he's damaged, we can fix him. We can plead with him to leave boys alone and go for girls. Let us fix our baby instead of killing him, please!" she pleaded.

They walked back into the living room, but their boy was gone. Against Akinlade's wishes, Kofoworola rushed towards the old van to search for him.

With his wife gone, Akinlade sank back into his brooding chair, the day's events swirling in his head like dust kicked up by the wind. He remembered the shocking moment when he walked in on Jide and Wale; his first impulse had been to rush to the backyard, pick up a cutlass, and chop off their heads right there and then, but the boys ran out before he could carry out the deed. He remembered how he had walked the thin lines of sanity and insanity the entire afternoon, with moments of inexplicable excitement where he would laugh derisively for no reason at all, followed by extensive moments of silence and great depression. He remembered how his son had had the nerve to return to the house a few hours later.

Jide had come in with his own key and found his father home alone in his favourite chair, staring at blanks. He passed by the man as if he were invisible, went to his room, and returned with a bag. He was about to leave the house when his father grabbed him by the hand.

"Son, what appeals to you in the body of a man? Really? Is it the ruggedness and flatness of his chest or the straight lines he calls a body that causes your manhood to rise like flour to yeast?"

"Dad, I love Wale deeply."

"Love? What do you know about love? What sort of despicable, reprehensible love means sleeping bone-to-bone with another man? Have you ever been with a woman?" The father asked his son.

"No!" he replied unapologetically.

The father looked at his son and shook his head.

"You have never tried loving a woman? You do not know what it feels like to let a woman's lips brush against yours? You cannot begin to imagine the excitement you'll feel when her naked and tender breasts are nestled in your hands, son. Have you ever buried your head in a woman's breasts and just watched all your problems melt away like butter on fire? Do you know how unbelievably happy you would be when you run your hands around the elegant curves of a woman's body or how indescribably thrilling it is to carefully sweep your fingers up her thighs to feel her wetness? If you have never tasted honey, how can you even dare to call it bitter?"

"My heart does not race when a woman smiles at me, but it flips over a million times when Wale does. That's how I know, dad."

"Wale? Same Wale, who suffered from skin disease all through his childhood? Same Wale, who does not know his left from his right? If you must eat a toad, could you not at least eat a super-fat and juicy one? You had to pick that moron?"

"He is the one my heart craves, dad."

"Then, perhaps it is not you who are stupid, but your heart. Son, we are Africans. In Africa, opposites attract—a bull to a cow, a dog to a bitch, a cock to a hen—it can never be any other way! A man bonking another man is simply not our culture. It is taboo! Leave Wale and all other boys alone so I can still call you son or stick with him and cease to be my son, all your inheritance with it."

The young man had given his father a cold stare, dusted his feet on the welcome mat outside the door, and walked away. The old man shook his head in pity and sank back into his trance.

***

Kofoworola's breasts were heavy and painful. The pain felt like needles thrusting through her breasts, but what bothered her the most was that she had driven around the entire neighbourhood with no glimpse of her son. She attempted to call him multiple times, but his phone was turned off. It was almost eleven now, and although her heart urged her to keep driving until she found her son, her mind knew it was wiser to go home.

A few streets before theirs, she saw many people gathered around a bonfire, excitedly taking pictures with their camera phones, but she was too disturbed and pained to share in their excitement as she headed home.

When she first saw the door, her heart stopped beating briefly. She remembered locking it before she drove out, but now it stood yawning wide at that ungodly hour! As she moved towards the door, a sudden sense of unease washed over her. With every step, the air seemed heavier and suffocating.

As soon as she got into the living room, she let out a blood-curdling scream before collapsing to the floor in a trembling heap.

The needles that were poking at her breasts moved to her heart first and gradually spread all over her body. She was on fire! She threw off her scarf, threw off her wrapper, and ran her hands all over her body like someone demented. The fire she felt in her body coursed through her veins, and she wanted to die. She needed to die! There was absolutely no way she would stick around to clean up the mess her family had created. So, she picked up the gun, grateful they had saved her some bullets. She was about to have her brains mess up the tiles like her son did when, suddenly, her husband groaned and lifted a blood-soaked hand to stop her. This was one problem he knew he could not dream away—not this time!

He quickly ran towards his wife, pried the gun out of her hands, and held her tightly as she gnashed her teeth. He knew the days ahead would be cruelly dark. He knew he would have to spend the rest of his life convincing his wife that he did not kill their only son. Indeed, grief had murdered him. His Wale had fallen prey to the wrath of an anti-gay mob who pierced his anus with a red-hot fork before setting him ablaze. Akinlade knew he would have to convince her that he had no hand in that either, just as he had tried to explain to their boy when he charged into the house, calling him a monster for doing something so despicable to Wale. He knew that he would also have to convince her that, despite all he had said earlier, the heavy hand of death upon his household and the pitch-black darkness it dragged along with it had brought him some strange clarity. He now wishes none of it had happened. Nothing seemed to matter to him now. It did not matter if their boy liked men, women, or both. No matter his regrets, he knew that what was done was done. He, therefore, held onto his wife more tightly as her eyes bled to the floor and waited patiently for time to sweep away the gloom hovering around his home like a dark bird of prey.

The Pastor and The Robber

Pastor Gbenga slammed the door as soon as he got home that night, as if it were the cause of his terrible day. He kicked the door again and again to let out some of his frustration, yet his anger boiled over like a kettle left for too long on a stove. The weight of the day's disappointment pressed down on him like a sack of stones borne by weary shoulders. It had been the most difficult day since he started preaching in buses at Orisha Motor Park two months ago. Business was not good at all today. He had preached on sowing and reaping, seed time and harvest, the joy, beauty, and reward that came with giving, and everything else he could think of to compel his audience to give, but nothing worked. The words simply fell to the ground, where they were crushed by thorns. In a desperate attempt to stir some response, he even organised a deliverance session on one of the buses, hoping to change the people's minds, but still, nothing! He had exhausted every tactic except using a crowbar to pry the money from the people's clenched fists. Other days had been okay. At least when it was terrible, some people still gave him a little money for his effort. Today, the people's hearts were stones.

Adding insult to injury, the boys who ran the park insisted that he pay them their commission. Whether business was good or not, he had to renew his daily subscription, or else he would not be allowed miles around the park. So, today was a loss-making day.

With a heavy heart, Pastor Gbenga locked the door behind him and tossed the keys into a corner of the room. Then, he gulped down some liquid, hoping to drown out the day's troubles, and then went straight to bed to sleep out the depression, but he could not sleep. His mind kept wandering off to the days he spent in the village. He shook his head at his journey. He had truly known hunger in his lifetime. His parents were poor farmers, residing in a small farmhouse in their village. Their lives were marked by hardship and struggle, with every meal earned through sweat and hard work.

The burden of his past experiences mingled with the difficulties of the present as he lay in bed, creating a complex web of emotions that would not go away. His mind was stuck on the recollections of his lowly beginnings no matter how hard he tried to drift off to sleep.

As a young boy, Gbenga Adelaja dreamed of escaping the stinging bite of poverty in the village and enjoying the luxury he had heard of in big cities like Lagos. It was a dream of escape, of breaking free from the stifling embrace of poverty that seemed to suffocate every corner of his existence. He knew the only way he could escape from the shackles of poverty was through education. So, he went to the local elementary school and pursued his studies with determination, much to the dismay of his father, whose hardened gaze bore the weight of generations of struggle. To him, education was a complete waste of precious time. He considered it a frivolous distraction from the harsh realities of survival. Gbenga was reprimanded by his father every time he picked up his school bag to head to school, but he clung to his dream because he believed that education was the only path to a better life. On weekends, however, he helped his parents on their small piece of land, which was their only source of livelihood. During the weekdays, his father worked at Peter Eze's father's timber shop, hoping to bring more income home, but that was yet to happen. The small farm, therefore, determined if they would have food in their stomachs or if they would go hungry. Every harvest, they would keep a few items to feed on and sell off the rest at the village market.

During the festive seasons, when the city boys descended upon the village like royalty, Gbenga watched with envy and fascination as they flaunted the latest fashions, displaying their shiny new toys and textbooks with a carefree confidence that appeared unreal compared to his own life, which was being smothered by poverty and lack.

The city boys and their belongings drew Gbenga in like a moth to a flame, despite the jealousy that gnawed at his heart. He yearned to turn the pages of their textbooks and lose himself in the knowledge they carried. So, he took advantage of any chance he got to run errands for them, so he could peek at their books and learn a small portion of what they knew. It was a small price to pay in the face of his own lack. Every time he flipped through the pages of the borrowed textbooks under the shade of the *agbalumo* tree behind the battered walls of their home, Gbenga felt a glimmer of hope come alive within him—the conviction that one day, he too would be able to pursue education and open the doors to a better future in the city.

Ah, education—the key to wealth and success! Gbenga was determined to get educated no matter the cost, even if he had to sell his blood to get it. He swore he would get educated and meant every word of it. But life, like a mischievous chef, had a way of mixing up the menu and muddling one's order. One could request a steaming cup of opportunity but be served an unsweetened bowl of disappointment instead.

The last time he was within the walls of a school was when he collected his WAEC result. He had walked through the community secondary school gate with so much anxiety, even though he was confident he studied hard and wrote the final exams well. He knew that many things could go wrong—from withheld results, to cancelled results, to missing results, or a woeful failure of students at some exam centres because their coordinators failed to 'see' the exam officials. One could never tell how the dice would roll. So, he joined the others with his heart in his mouth to queue in front of the principal's office for their results.

As the line inched forward, Gbenga felt a sense of dread mixed with a glimmer of hope. No matter how hard he tried, his heart could not stop running one hundred kilometres per second, and his palms could not stop sweating. He rubbed them off on his khaki shorts several times in a futile attempt to keep them dry. It did not help that most of his schoolmates who came out of the principal's office were in tears. Some collapsed to the ground, their cries echoing through the air like a funeral dirge, while others simply limped away, crushed by the verdict they had just received. The intensity of the moment, combined with the oppressive heat of the midday sun, started to snuff life out of Gbenga when suddenly, the principal's voice rang resonantly like the school bell.

"Gbenga Adelaja!"

It was eventually his turn. Immediately after he heard his name, time froze. His heart stopped beating, and he died for a minute. The outcome of this singular moment would determine the path of his entire existence. Everything depended on this moment—everything! Gbenga's mind raced with visions of his future, each possibility more vivid and stark than the last. Would he rise to the heights of success, living in a grand mansion with maids and servants at his every beck and call? Or would he be condemned to a life of toil, pushing a wheelbarrow around the filthy local market, earning peanuts for each day's sweat, his dreams shattered and his spirit broken? And what about love? Would he marry the prettiest girl in town with skin as soft and as smooth as silk and her laughter like a sonorous song to his ears? Or would it be ugly Risi, who hawked akara around the neighbourhood, her face covered with lumps as big as fists, and her existence evidence of the harsh realities of life's cruelty? In that fleeting moment, the choice between prosperity and poverty, love and loneliness, lay unsteadily perched on the edge of possibility.

Gbenga walked into the principal's office with shaky feet and dripping palms. It was a large and very plain office, except for the painting on the wall with the inscription:

Life is like a parade ground,

Where at the shout of 'About Turn!'

The last takes the lead.

The words made goosebumps crawl all over his skin. If life were indeed a parade ground, prone to sudden changes like a windstorm, what then would be his fate? In his case, he had always been at the top of his class, and his academic prowess was a source of personal pride and validation. What if there was a sudden shout of "About Turn!" and he was swiftly moved to the bottom of the class, his hard-earned achievements rendered useless instantly? The idea made him shiver with fear.

"Gbenga!" the principal's voice cut through his thoughts. "I'm afraid I have both good and bad news," he continued. I'll give you the good news first." With steady hands, the principal reached for a small piece of paper, his expression unreadable as he scribbled something down from a large sheet. Gbenga's heart raced with a thousand possibilities as he watched.

"Here is your result. Congratulations!" he declared, his words echoing through the room like the triumphant beats of a village drum.

Gbenga stared at the piece of paper with utter relief and joy. For a moment, he floated into the skies out of sheer excitement—excitement much greater than he could contain. He wanted to jump at the principal but stopped in his tracks, not knowing how he might react; he was, after all, still the revered principal, excellent exam result or not. So, he controlled himself. He would scream and go wild with excitement when he stepped out of the principal's office.

"Now the bad news..." the principal cut into his excitement. "With the sort of grades you have, you ought to qualify for a scholarship for the state university, which is what I believe you were hoping for. Unfortunately, this year, the school has decided to take turns awarding scholarships to students based on the village they came from. You see, some villages complained that they may never get the chance to benefit from the scholarship scheme if it was based on merit alone. Since it is supposed to be a community development scheme, and since the funds come from the entire nine villages, it was agreed that there should be some form of roster where the best from each village gets awarded each year."

"Sir, does that mean I can apply for the exams again next year?"

"I'm afraid not. Your village, Agbogiri Village, is the ninth on the list, meaning a person from your village can only be considered for the scholarship in nine years."

In that instant, Gbenga watched his lofty dream of making it big in life fly out the principal's tiny window. The joy that had enveloped him just moments before vanished into the air, leaving a sense of despair as deep as the darkest night.

The weeks that followed the principal's announcement found Gbenga wallowing in devastating depression. He did not eat at all, and when his mother forced the cocoyam down his throat, it came right back up. Afraid that the young lad would die under their watch if they did not do something drastic to help him, they sent him to the city to serve as a houseboy to one of his uncles, who promised to support the boy in his quest for education. Gbenga was filled with hope once again.

Ten years slipped by like grains of sand through Gbenga's weary fingers, leaving him trapped in a fancy cage of unfulfilled promises and shattered dreams. Despite living in an opulent house filled with all the fine things of life, Gbenga remained a reflection of poverty—lean, worn, and weary from the endless toil that ate up his days.

Each time he dared to bring up the subject of education, his uncle would brush it aside flippantly with a wave of the hand and promise to enrol him during the next session, the next session, and the next session, and then the session after that. This continued until it became painfully clear to Gbenga that the man had no intention of ever fulfilling his promise to him and his parents—he had been betrayed! His dream of becoming educated and climbing to the pinnacle of success had once again been shattered like a clay pot hit by lightning.

The young man knew then that he had to go into the streets of Lagos to carve out his own destiny rather than relying on others to do it for him, but he was too afraid to venture out. The streets of Lagos called out to him, offering him freedom and opportunities for a better life, but the thought of fleeing the familiar for the unfamiliar made him terribly afraid. Each day, as his uncle stepped out of the opulent mansion, Gbenga would stand by the massive gate, his small bag from ten years ago clutched tightly under his armpit, only to be paralysed by the overwhelming weight of uncertainty. Where would he stay? How would he feed? These questions ate his mind and kept him frozen behind the imposing gates of his uncle's mansion—a prisoner of his own fear and doubt.

On a day when the sun burned with fury, he met Pastor Kayode on a bus ride home from Ikorodu Market, where his uncle had sent him to pick up some items for his warehouse. Pastor Kayode hopped onto the bus as soon as it was fully loaded and navigated out of the park. He quickly introduced himself and prayed for the passengers, waving a Bible nearly the size of the bus in the air. He then shared some passages from the scriptures, with his voice rising above the noise in the crowded bus. The words resonated with most of the passengers as they nodded with occasional sighs and grunts. Pastor Kayode finished by appealing to the passengers to support God's work and contribute to advancing His ministry so that they may reap the harvests that come with sowing. The bus echoed with his passionate plea. As the people dug into their pockets and purses to bring out generous donations, a light bulb lit deep within Gbenga's soul.

The next day, armed with the few naira notes he had gathered from Uncle Bode's many errands, he embarked on a journey to Orisha Motor Park on the other side of Lagos—a path he knew his uncle would never tread. From that moment onward, Gbenga never looked back, especially as business had been relatively okay, allowing him to always have food in his stomach and a roof over his head within just a month. But today had been so unkind, bringing tight-fisted customers his way.

In the middle of the night, he heard a dog barking hungrily in the neighbourhood. He stirred, sleepy-eyed, as he felt his stomach barking bitterly, too. Feeling tired and frustrated, a silly thought crossed his mind—perhaps he should convince the dog to offer itself as a willing sacrifice to him to appease his own hunger, as it did not make any sense that they were both hungry. He quickly dismissed the idea as foolishness and then shifted restlessly on his flat and worn-out mattress for a comfortable position in search of sleep. He stirred again, ignored the growling of his stomach, cursed his ill luck, and slept off, surprisingly sound.

***

The robber was as pissed as hell! His bike suddenly coughed to a halt around a dead neighbourhood on his way to his Canaan Land, where milk and honey flowed abundantly. The rich would have gathered their harvest during the day, awaiting his visit at night. All he needed to do now was honour their invitation.

"But this *yeye* bike! This stupid *yeye* bike!" he cursed under his breath.

He looked around him; the neighbourhood he was stuck in bore no promises. Maybe he should look around again. Who knew if he might just be lucky? Sometimes, gold could be hidden amidst cow dung.

He found a house with a flowery hedge and reasoned that stealing a phone or two and maybe a laptop could very well cover the cost of fixing his bike the following morning. So, he jumped over the hedge.

A silly dog started to bark. He thought to silence it for good but did not want to alert anyone, so he ignored it. The dog sounded too hungry and looked too tired to attack him anyway.

He got to the door and thought to knock it down. Heck! He had a gun—a fully loaded one at that. He could very well afford to spray the entire neighbourhood if they dared accost him, but he would rather that did not happen. It was meant to be a quick robbery; take what needs to be taken and shoot anyone who stands in the way! So, he decided to use the ceiling instead. He found an opening, and with one leap, he was in the ceiling.

He thought about scorpions or maybe a snake biting him and how it would make him cry like a baby! He shook his head at the thought. A weeping armed robber? Not good! Not good at all! So, he scanned the place with his little searchlight before advancing.

He found another end opening and landed with a thud, pausing to ensure he had not alerted anyone.

To his dismay, the room he landed in was bare, with absolutely nothing in it except for the flat mattress where a sickly-looking man lay, snoring. He did not know which infuriated him the more—that he risked his life and burned so much energy all for nothing, or that the man could still sleep and snore in such abject poverty! He checked around the even flatter pillow upon which the man rested his head, drooling from both corners of his mouth in deep slumber.

No phone! None whatsoever! What sort of dead meat did not own a phone?

He got so mad that he considered doing the man a favour by saving him from his miserable existence. So, he took out his gun from underneath his jacket, cocked it, and was about to fire when he noticed a Bible on the floor beside the mattress. That got him even angrier, so he aimed his gun, ready to fire!

'Make I scatter dis modafucker's brains, use am help am paint this modafucking walls!' He thought, fuming.

Suddenly, something caught his eye that stopped him in his tracks. Right above the snoring man's head was a half-empty bottle of *shekpe*. He chuckled hoarsely and shook his head as he picked up the bottle, uncorked it, took a sip, looked up at the ceiling where he had come in, shook his head again, and then sat on the floor to finish the drink, with his gun beside him.

Pastor Gbenga slowly opened his eyes to the blinding morning sun streaming through his bare window. The sharp sting made him shut them quickly. Bitterness built up in his mouth when he remembered that his throat was as dry as his pockets. He reached for the bottle he had left over his head the night before, but his hand grasped nothing. That awakened him fully because he was sure he had left it there. He tried to steady his eyes and got up to search properly for his bottle. His search was cut short when he noticed a figure hovering over him and casting a shadow across the room.

He dropped to the ground, face down, whimpering and peeing in his pants as he begged for mercy. "I... I... b... beg you in the... the name of G... God, please don't kill me. Take anything you... you want..." he stuttered, trembling like a reed in the wind.

"Shut up ya mouth dia! Stand up!" the robber yelled. Pastor Gbenga stood up, trying desperately to hide his wet mid-section with one hand and cover his eyes with the other.

"Open those ya eyes dia!" the robber ordered, and the pastor obeyed.

Pastor Gbenga looked upon the tall figure of the robber standing before him with enormous trepidation. His heart skipped a few beats as he took in the menacing presence, wondering if it was the gun next to him that made his height so intimidating.

Despite how terrified he was, Pastor Gbenga did not fail to notice how young the intruder was—perhaps not much older than nineteen. He wondered how someone so young could emit such an air of intimidation.

"Oya, look around you. Anything dey hia wey person fit tif?" the robber asked, his eyes scanning the room alongside its other occupant. "Well..." he continued, "I no fit suffer the kain suffer wey I suffer take enta hia to take comot all for nothing!" His voice was cold and menacing, sending shivers down the pastor's spine. "So, abeg, wia you keep key? I wan comot!" he said while lighting a cigarette.

The pastor quickly scanned the room, trembling as he ran to pick up the key where he had flung it angrily the night before. He opened the door with great trepidation to let the robber out. To his surprise, as the robber was leaving, he reached into his pocket, took out a rumpled five-hundred-naira note, and stretched it to the pastor with an unexpected gesture of generosity.

Pastor Gbenga was caught off guard by the robber's sudden act of kindness and was both relieved and confused, wondering if it was a test of some sort. What if he stretched out his hand to receive the gift but received a bullet right on the bridge that separated his eyes instead? But then, what if it was not a test? He would have missed out on the only hope for a meal for the day. So, he shakily accepted the offer.

"See ba, na street all of us dey. Na the same struggle the two of us dey. So, take dis money. Hol am make you at least fit buy garri, make I see something wack next time wen I come!"

With a gentle pat on the pastor's back, the robber eased out of the house, his gun swaying menacingly at his hip.

***

That morning, business boomed!

Pastor Gbenga gave a testimony to the passengers. He recounted the story of his encounter with the robber, describing himself as bold and ferocious as a lion. He brazenly told them about how he dared the intruder to lay a finger on the abundance God had graciously blessed him with and how the robber, out of fear, gave him all he had on him instead. It was the ultimate power of God at work, and they had to sow into his life if they wanted to experience such miracles.

And the people sowed bountifully!

The Fear of Darkness

A Sequel to **"The Pastor and the Robber"**

The people were afraid; yes, they were. They had been taught that life held a more profound spiritual dimension beyond the physical realm, which they found difficult to comprehend. While they could see and make sense of the physical world, the spiritual realm remained elusive and mysterious. It was described to them as vast, sinister, and beyond comprehension. Many among them harboured a fear of darkness and felt intimidated by the uncertainties of the unknown.

In the whispers of the night, the people learned of the intricate dance between mortals and spirits on the earthly stage. They were told of a realm where humanity stumbled in darkness, ensnared by unseen threads spun by delicate weavers, oblivious to the malevolent spirits lurking in the shadows. These spirits, it was said, ceaselessly conspired and connived, weaving webs of cruelty to entangle the naive. Not all spirits were benevolent, they were told. Many were whispered to be vile, bloodthirsty entities, relentless in their pursuit to cause mischief and harm. To shield themselves from such dark forces, the people were urged to cling steadfastly to the wisdom of the oracle—the eye of the gods and the divine conduit through which the spirits whispered their secrets to mortal ears.

Pastor Gbenga was no stranger to the fears that haunted the hearts of the people. Despite lacking formal education, he possessed a keen insight into the human mind. He knew how to exert the power of belief to gently guide his followers towards his own agenda. Like a master puppeteer pulling invisible strings, he manipulated their deepest anxieties and shaped their perceptions to align with his teachings. To them, he was the oracle—the conduit to the divine and the voice of wisdom in a world plagued by uncertainties.

After the breakthrough at Orisha Motor Park, he founded a church underneath the generous shade of a mango tree with only six faithful followers. He knew a mere six congregants would not usher him into the promised land he always dreamed of or anywhere near Canaan's shore. So he immersed himself in scripture and fervently prayed for a divine intervention that would elevate him from zero to hero. As Brother Emeka led the congregation in praise and worship that Sunday morning, he lifted his head to the heavens for a sign.

"God, you know I never asked to be born, but I'm here now. Please be merciful, and do not let me starve to death. Look at me, Lord. Men my age already have wives and even children, but how can I provide for a wife with these hungry followers you have given me? Look at them; they are so hungry and poor that my fists can rest comfortably in the hollows beneath their eyes. I can see every vein in their flesh and even count their bones. They are waiting for crumbs to fall from my table so they can eat. Lord, I need people whose table I can sit at, not ones who sit at mine. Please do something to change this situation, Lord, and I promise I won't bother you ever again."

While he was still praying, pandemonium struck the church. He heard a woman's wailing and men's murmuring.

He opened his eyes to see what was causing the commotion.

Is it the tax force again? He feared. He had told them several times that he operated a church, not a business centre, and churches do not pay taxes. His church may be under a tree, but he had as much right as those other overly pompous preachers who preached in large auditoriums and owned private jets. They were not bothered by taxes, so why should they bother him? Was it not the same gospel of truth they preached?

Thankfully, it was not the tax force. Four heavily built men brought in a teenage girl, followed by a woman who, by her distraught cries and the way she called out the girl's name, seemed to be her mother. The girl convulsed, thrashing about and frothing at the mouth as they placed her at his feet.

His team of six, consisting of four women and two men, stood frozen, mouths agape, shock and fear etched on their faces. One of them snapped out of it and darted off like a headless chicken in search of water to pour on the girl. His sudden movement jolted the others into action, and they rushed to join him, their screams mingling with the girl's mother's inconsolable wails.

"Pastor, you have to heal this girl, or else she will die!"

"No, I can't heal her," he said flatly.

"Huh?" the people chorused, disbelief written all over their faces."

"Only God can heal, so pray and channel your faith. Believe it can happen, and it will," he said. He looked at the weeping mother, who was now crouched beside her sick child. "Look, Madam," he continued, "do you believe in God?" The woman nodded in the affirmative, trying hard to stop the tears. "If you do, then you should know that now is not the time to cry but to pray. It's the biggest sign of doubt and unbelief when we have problems and cry instead of praying. Therefore, if I so much as hear a sniff from you, you'll have to carry your child out of my church. Do you understand?"

"Yes, sir! Yes, sir!" the woman quickly nodded, wiping her eyes and nose.

"Okay, good. Now, my job is to pray, and yours is to believe. If I pray and you do not believe, then this girl dies."

"Ehn?" the woman shrieked.

"You would have killed your own child. Do you understand?"

"Yes, sir! Yes, sir! I believe. I believe. I believe o!" the woman cried, throwing her arms in the air in total surrender.

"Okay, good. Now, pray like you believe!"

The woman started praying in various incoherent languages while the pastor urgently called for his anointing oil and a spoon. His followers hurried to fetch the items. By now, a small crowd had gathered under the tree, some out of curiosity, to witness the unfolding events. Others, weary of their own impoverished lives, looked on with disinterest.

He took the oil and the spoon, opened the bottle, and held it up to the heavens. "Father!" he exclaimed, "do not let darkness overshadow light. Do not let the marine spirits that have taken over this girl succeed."

As soon as his audience heard 'marine spirits', some moved backwards, perhaps fearing the spirits might jump out to attack or possess them as well. Others intensified their prayers, screaming the words in hopes that God would hear them and the demons would flee as well once the screams masked their apparent fear and lent more authority to their voices.

"Prove now that you're God!" he prayed, looking up at the sky and winking at God. Then he started to sing and dance around the frothing girl.

The walls of Jericho fell down flat.

The walls of Jericho fell down flat.

As the children of God were praising the Lord,

The walls of Jericho fell down flat.

He poured some oil onto the spoon, held the girl's head on his thighs, forced her already locked teeth open with the spoon, and left it there.

"Let us begin to pray!" he yelled at the crowd, who seemed to have forgotten about the marine spirits lurking around and had reduced the intensity of their prayers.

"Pray! For we wrestle not against flesh and blood but against principalities and powers, and in this case, marine spirits of the highest order. Pray! I see the queen of the coast rising in anger. She is screaming wildly! I see fire burning her body. Yes! The Holy Ghost fire burns even in the deepest ocean. Pray! She is coming! She is trying to get out of the water! She is coming for this girl here! Pray that she dies in the water and this girl gets her freedom!"

The crowd fervently engaged in prayers, their eyes firmly closed. Some prayed vigorously with their hands and legs, as if repelling the unseen spirits that surrounded them. They marched like soldiers, aiming to crush the demons underfoot, waved their hands in the air to confront those above, and rolled on the ground to reinforce the effort. Some cried out, seeking mercy from the demons, while others shouted louder, asserting their authority over evil forces.

Meanwhile, Pastor Gbenga focused intently on the girl, hoping for any sign of improvement. It appeared their prayers were falling short, and a sense of worry and fear crept over him. Throughout his time as a pastor, he had never been called upon to perform a healing, yet he knew he could not claim to be a genuine servant of

God if he could not invoke divine intervention to heal the sick girl. In today's world, mere words of faith were not always enough; people yearned for tangible miracles—things they could see with their own eyes. He realised that the outcome of this moment could either cement his reputation as the influential pastor he aspired to be or crush his ambitions before they could even blossom. This was the pivotal moment he had been praying for—a moment that could change his life forever!

Perhaps, in an unexpected turn of events, God decided that He had been vigilant for far too long and deserved a brief break—a break that could abruptly halt Pastor Gbenga's career with the swiftness of a finger snap. The pastor could not bear the thought of God abandoning him now and pondered what the Almighty might be contemplating above.

Did He see through me to realise I am a fraud? He wondered. No! I am not a fraud! I am just someone to whom life has handed peppers and who desperately needs to make pepper soup.

Pastor Gbenga knew that if God did not show up, he and his unborn generations would face starvation. He might have stumbled into this life, but it was all he had now. There was no turning back. He could not return to the village to harvest cocoyams and palm oil with his elderly parents and younger siblings, not when they relied on him to find wealth in the city and send some money back home. He also could not risk returning to his uncle's house to face a lifetime of servitude.

God just had to save him. He might not have been entirely honest, but at least he was not causing anyone harm. After all, he was expanding the Kingdom of Heaven and even trying to heal the sick. That was something commendable—even God should be proud.

He glanced at the crowd as they fervently prayed, already

imagining the disappointment that would cloud their faces if the girl failed to recover. For a fleeting moment, he pictured them showering him with abundant cash, only to come back one by one to reclaim their offerings until he was left with nothing!

"God! Prove now that you are God!" he screamed at the heavens, desperation in his voice.

To Pastor Gbenga's astonishment, the girl rose to her feet, took the spoon out of her mouth, wiped the saliva from her lips with the hem of her dress, and surveyed her surroundings, searching for a familiar face among the crowd. Soon, she spotted her mother kneeling beside her, praying fervently. She called out her name and gently touched her.

The woman screamed with joy and rejoicing, embracing the child so tightly that the girl winced in pain. The crowd erupted in wild excitement, and some of the idle young men who had been lingering around to witness the outcome rushed to the pastor, hoisting him onto their shoulders and singing his praises.

Pastor Gbenga enjoyed the ride, the attention, the triumph, and the glory for a few minutes. Then he shouted angrily, "Put me down this minute! It is not I who healed this girl, but God Almighty, and only He should receive all the praise! I am only a vessel used by the Most High God. I am His oracle. I am His priest. A mere tool in His hands!"

The people went berserk with songs of praise, dancing with thunderous applause for God.

Immortal God, Invincible God,

Immortal God, how great thou art.

Immortal God, Invincible God,

Immortal God, how great thou art.

Oh, that men would praise the Lord,

Oh, that men would praise the Lord,

For His goodness and for His wonderful works

To the children of men,

To the children of men,

For His goodness and for His wonderful works

To the children of men,

To the children of men.

He has broken the gates of brass,

And cut the bars of iron asunder,

He has broken the gates of brass,

And cut the bars of iron asunder.

The crowd sang and danced and went into a frenzy when the pastor started to sing *'The Walls of Jericho'* chorus again.

"Thanksgiving offering basket!" Pastor Gbenga's voice rang out beneath the sprawling branches of the mango tree. An excited usher rushed forward in response, carrying the basket so that the congregation could give what their hearts desired. As they dug into their pockets and purses to contribute what they could in thanksgiving for the blessing they had received, the air was charged with excitement. Everyone gave according to their means and the urging of their spirit during this act of collective giving.

Pastor Gbenga winked, thankfully, at God. He watched the basket go around with a sense of satisfaction, knowing that the gifts offered would ease his suffering and bring him closer to his dream of becoming stupendously rich.

News of the miracle spread rapidly through various channels, each offering a different version of events. However, they all shared one common theme: Pastor Gbenga Adelaja was the new wonder worker in town! Some accounts claimed he brought a dead girl back to life, while others suggested he engaged in physical combat with malevolent spirits until the girl was freed. Another variation insisted that the girl's entire family perished, only to be resurrected by Pastor Gbenga. Despite the discrepancies, Pastor Gbenga welcomed the attention, realising that any form of publicity, even if embellished, benefited him. After all, it drew crowds who were eager to witness the miracles attributed to him—the new wonder worker in town!

The pastor recognised that most of the crowd had gathered out of sheer curiosity, but he paid little mind to their motivations. This was his moment in the sun, and he intended to milk the situation until the cow squealed to death.

Fate seemed to be smiling upon him, as among the onlookers at the miraculous healing was Ifeanyi, a domestic worker employed by the local government chairman.

As soon as Ifeanyi returned home, he immediately called his colleagues to share the wonder he witnessed earlier in the day with them.

"O boy, una no see wetin my eye see today?"

"Wetin you see again, Ifeanyi? Your story no dey ever finish," one of his colleagues teased, though he and the others were eager to hear the tale Ifeanyi had to share.

"The thing wey my eye see korokoro, if nor be sey I take my two eyes see am, I for no ever believe sey e fit happen."

"Abeg talk wetin you see. If you no wan talk, carry dey go, make you no waste our time," another said, frustrated yet still eager to hear the story.

"Wait na. You too dey hurry. Relax, make I gist you," Ifeanyi said.

"That time wey Small Oga send me to go buy paper come ba, naim I say make I use chance take block Ifeoma, you know na," he continued, giving his colleagues a knowing look.

"Oh! So, na Ifeoma you go meet, wey you tell Big Oga sey na paper you find sotey, you miss for hours, wey you no come cook for Oga wen today na your turn to cook abi?" the first colleague questioned.

"Comot dia! You be police? Na you be Big Oga abi na Small Oga, abi you be the paper? I no dey even talk again sef," Ifeanyi said, feigning anger.

"Oya, oya, no vex. Talk. Wetin happen?" his colleagues pleaded.

"Ehen. As I been dey talk before somebody interrupt me. As I go see Ifeoma na, when we don do... you know, finish, naim she come dey escort me go where I go see okada to go buy Oga paper o. Naim we see sey crowd gather. I first think sey na two fighting. So, we say make we stay look small before I go buy the paper. As we reach na, na church wey dey under tree o. One girl been die and everybody dey cry as she be her mama only pikin, and the mama don old well well. Dem say she tey well well before she fit even born the girl sef. The only pikin wey person get for old age just die like that, hmmm!"

"Chei!"

"Hmmm!"

"Na wa o!" His colleagues exclaimed, hugging themselves and shaking their heads in deep sympathy for the poor woman who supposedly lost her only child at an old age.

"Naim pastor pull cloth!" Ifeanyi continued.

"Ehen!" his colleagues chorused, totally drawn into the story. "So, wetin come happen?"

"Pastor pull cloth, sey devu no fit snatch the girl life, sey e no dey possicant not when the girl don enter im church. Naim e begin dey pray! E begin dey pray. Naim one woman, wey follow carry the girl come, wey be the girl aunty come begin dey confess!"

"Ha!" his audience chorused, with shock and amazement evident on their faces.

"She begin confess sey she be mami water, sey na she kill the girl for their coven, sey na axe she knack for the girl head for their meeting wey come kill am for real life!"

"Ha!" his colleagues chorused again.

"People wicked for this world o," one said.

"Wetin the innocent girl do am na?" another asked.

"My brother, I no know o. If you ask me, na who I go ask? Na so me sef see am." Ifeanyi continued, "As she confess finish, naim the pastor come begin pray. E begin to pray, until the girl wey been don kpai kpatakpata jump up, begin shout say God don sew her head o! God don sew her head o!"

Ifeanyi's audience erupted into jubilation until they were

interrupted by their 'Big Oga', who had been eavesdropping the entire time.

"Ifeanyi! Where is the cup of tea that I asked you for? This is what you do, right? I pay you to watch movies in the streets when you are sent on errands, right?"

"No, Oga. I'm sorry, sir!"

"I know the right treatment for you. I will deal with you and your lead actor, the pastor. First thing tomorrow morning, go and get him here! Do you understand me?"

"Yes! Yes sir! Sorry sir!"

"If you wait for me to remind you tomorrow, I'll have you locked up and flogged mercilessly in the guardroom! Do you understand?"

"Yes, sir. I understand clearly, sir!"

With that, Big Oga walked away, leaving Ifeanyi visibly shaken. His boisterous audience had long dispersed as if they were never there.

At the break of dawn, Ifeanyi embarked on a quest to locate the pastor. Miraculously, upon reaching the mango tree, he stumbled upon a guide who seemed to know the pastor's house like the back of his hand, offering to lead him there without hesitation.

They arrived at the house and knocked on the front door.

"Yes, who is there?" a rather sleepy voice called out from within.

"It's me, sir," Ifeanyi answered.

"You, who?" the voice asked, irritated by the interruption of his sleep.

"Sir, my name is Ifeanyi. I work in the chairman's house, sir."

That got the man's attention inside, and his mind started to race. Which chairman? He thought. Only one man is called chairman around this vicinity.

If it was the one he thought it was, then what was his staff doing at his house, and so early in the morning?

"Which chairman?"

"The local government chairman, sir," Ifeanyi answered.

The words completely cleared the sleep from his eyes and voice, and he jumped out of bed to open the door.

"Erm, erm, good... good morning, sir. What can I do for you, please?" he asked the young boy, who wore a worried expression on his face.

"So sorry to bother you so early, sir. Ahm! My name, as I said earlier, is Ifeanyi—"

"Yes, yes, and you work for the local government chairman. So, what can I do for you?" he cut in, too anxious to let the man reintroduce himself.

"My oga said I should invite you over to his house."

Pastor Gbenga concealed his surprise. What could the local government chairman possibly want from him? Had he committed an offence? Was it regarding taxes again? Why could they not leave him alone in peace?

"Sir, he says you should come at once, sir," the boy said, still wearing an anxious expression.

For a minute, Pastor Gbenga wished he was being summoned

for something pleasant, but the look on the messenger's face wasn't exactly a 'something pleasant' one. He was certainly in trouble, and the poor boy only felt sorry for him. Whatever the case, he couldn't dare turn down the invitation, even if it were his life on the line. Not showing up would have put his life on the line anyway. So, he cleared his throat. "I hope there's no problem?"

"Err, no. No, sir. He just said he wants to see you."

"Okay, you'll need to give me some time so I can have a quick bath and dress up—"

"Ah! No, sir. Please, it is very urgent!"

From the panic in the boy's voice, Pastor Gbenga knew he could not push the issue further.

"Okay. Let me wash my face and put on something decent then."

"Okay, no problem, sir."

Pastor Gbenga had never met a dignitary such as the local government chairman before. He was unsure what to wear, but he knew that a man was mainly addressed as he was dressed. So, he washed and rinsed his face to look as tidy as possible. Then, he wore his Sunday best: a faded long-sleeve shirt that looked like it was white in its first life, his favourite trousers of the only two pairs he owned, and a brown, faded coat he inherited from an uncle who worked as a cook for a white man in their village. Next, he donned his only pair of shoes. They were battered and bruised around the heels, such that he appeared to be limping when he wore them. But he had already developed such a stylish manner of walking in them that everyone now assumed the limp was his natural sway.

Hopefully, the chairman will think so, too. But what did he really want to see him for? He knew he had gained some fame because of the signs and wonders he had recently performed, but the messenger's look was unpleasant. He was not expecting the chairman to be nice to him, and it was no news that the man was ruthless, even to his peers. What, then, would he do to him, a worthless nobody? The rich are typically not kind to the poor, he thought. Just as Peter Eze's father was never kind to his. His father worked in the man's timber shop for several years, and not once did he ever pay him their agreed-upon two thousand naira per month wage. Something always happened to shorten the meagre sum, and when his old man retired to the farms after over twenty years of service, the man accused him of stealing his money a week before his retirement and left his old man penniless.

Therefore, Pastor Gbenga expected no kind treatment from the rich; he braced up. After all, the eyes would never shed blood no matter what they saw. He would see the chairman and turn whatever the situation was to his advantage.

The chairman too, though a Muslim, must have his own fears of spirits and mammon too, Pastor Gbenga reasoned. He, too, most certainly must be afraid of the dark. Fear is a human vulnerability that even the most influential like the chairman might harbour. He too most likely had a fear of the supernatural—of spirits and demons lurking in the shadows. This fear of darkness, the pastor was eager to exploit. His mind ran a thousand miles per minute as he pondered how to leverage this shared human frailty to his advantage.

As Ifeanyi led him into the most magnificent building he had ever been in, Pastor Gbenga could feel it in his bones that his life was about to change forever. With every step he took through the opulent halls, he knew he was stepping into a new chapter of his life. For a split second, his mind wandered to the principal's office in his village, where he had watched his younger self fill up with hope for the future, only for it to be abruptly snatched away. Fear crept up on him momentarily as he walked behind Ifeanyi to see the chairman, but he quickly braced himself. He was not about to let the fear and disappointments of the past steal this moment from him. He therefore allowed himself to feel the excitement of the moment as anticipation buzzed like a swarm of bees in the air around him. He stood still for a moment and drew in as much of the air as his lungs could take. When he started to walk again, he was certain it was the beginning of an extraordinary journey that would shape his life in ways he could not yet imagine.

More on Pastor Gbenga in: Pastor Gbenga's Chronicles.

The Riverbank

Based on a True Account

I read Buchi Emecheta's book, *The Joys of Motherhood*, nearly twenty years ago when I was only fourteen, yet its words clawed at the recesses of my mind every time my older sister, Obiageli, visited. The book tells the tale of Nnu Ego, who lived a relatively impoverished and turbulent life and sacrificed all for her children, only to die alone by the roadside and then be rewarded with a costly funeral for all her sacrifices as a mother. What is the joy in that? What is the use of a costly funeral cloth for a woman who wore the rags of poverty all her life?

No matter how hard I tried, the letters in the book would not leave my head. I remembered every word written in it; all its letters and punctuation marks stood in bold prints on the screen of my mind. But why did the book occupy so much space in my head whenever Obiageli whisked through my door? Could it be because she badgered me about giving my daughter, Nwakaego, a playmate?

I stopped stirring the meat I was frying to quickly check up on my only child in the living room. I knew she was safe in her playpen, but I still worried about all the what-ifs that could happen once I took my eyes off her for a second.

What if?

What if she choked on her own saliva?

What if she suddenly caught a cold on a sunny day while I was too preoccupied with frying meat for the restaurant's use the next day to ensure she stayed warm?

What if the playpen suddenly broke a leg, and she tumbled out and broke her neck?

What if?

Oh! What if?

I raced into the living room, praying earnestly that none of the many what-ifs in my head became my reality. I would die if anything happened to my little girl!

There she was! My precious daughter, Nwakaego! She was safe, thankfully. I placed the back of my right hand across her forehead. She was neither cold nor hot. I heaved a deep sigh of relief. She was not choking on her saliva, and her playpen still looked sturdy, so I could rest easy knowing it would not break anytime soon—even though I would still worry. I picked my eight-month-old daughter up and examined her body in case an insect bit her in the last two minutes that I was away, but she looked fine. She was fine. Everything was fine except for her eyes. Her eyes looked sad.

She was nibbling on a toy, as she had done since she started teething, but it looked like the toy or the relief from chewing on it bored her or gave her no pleasure whatsoever.

Could Obiageli be right? Is my daughter lonely? Why does she always have this sad look? I wondered.

I remember the last time Nwakaego's face lit up was when Obiageli visited with her six children. Ah, yes! Six children! Her first child, Adaobi, brought her the joy of motherhood. Her second daughter, Chioma, was born so Adaobi could have a companion. Nkiruka, her third daughter, came into the world unexpectedly after a mishap with a broken condom. Uchechi, her fourth child, was intended to be a son, but an old woman supposedly turned him into a girl in the ninth month of her pregnancy. Obiageli swears that the switch happened at the market when the old woman, whom she insists is a witch, bumped into her and hit her protruding belly with hers. Her fifth child, Obinna, proved that she, too, could have a male child. And Obika, her sixth child, came so Obinna would have a brother to 'gist' with.

Obiageli was pregnant again, and only she could tell what purpose this child would serve. Yes, Obiageli already has six good-looking, yet malnourished, children who know how to cheer up my daughter.

Whenever her cousins visit, Nwakaego's laughter and joyful leaps greet them as they enter. She relishes the opportunity to chase them around on all fours. But once their visit ends, she retreats into herself, her eyes clouded with a sadness that lingers long after they depart.

It made me conclude that Obiageli was right! Nwakaego was lonely!

For a minute, I was angry. Why was I not enough for her? I spent every waking moment with her, juggling running the restaurant business and being her best friend. Why was that not enough?

Then, I thought about Nduka, my husband. Three years ago, before we got married, we agreed to have only one child. He firmly believes that no woman should endure the strain of pregnancy and childbirth more than once. So, after Nwakaego's birth, I accepted my role in caring for her, content in knowing she would be our only child. How could I now approach him to advocate for a second child to ensure our daughter's happiness?

Okay, there is nothing to worry about! In a few months, she will start school and mix up with many children her age, and everything will be fine, I told myself.

But just then, I relived one of my many conversations with Obiageli about the issue.

"Chiamaka, how many Igbo... no... African men do you see content and happy to have only one child?"

"Well, Nduka is one of the few I know!" I replied, trying to keep my cool.

"Really?" she asked quizzically.

I affirmed. "He doesn't want me to go through the hassles of pregnancy and delivery a second time."

"Wehdone ma! Queen Amina of Zaria! He might as well stop your monthly guest as well na. Or is that one not stressful, too?" she asked, placing both arms over her hips like someone ready for battle.

I would have said she was jealous if I did not know her any better.

"How many Igbo men do you see who are happy to have one child, a female child, for that matter?" she continued. "See, the woman who has only a female child might as well be barren!"

Oh no! She did not! She is my older sister, and I am expected to respect her, but she should not push it!

"So, female children are not children, eh?" I snapped, failing to hide my anger.

"I didn't say they are not children o. What I mean is, in the eyes of the world, especially in the eyes of your in-laws, you are a barren woman if you have only female children."

I could not believe my ears. "You went to school, Oby. This is the twenty-first century, for goodness' sake! Female children are just as important as male children!"

"That's my problem with you, Chiamaka! What does school have to do with it? The same school where you draw and label cockroaches and grasshoppers up and down, then use what's left of the time to look for X that is forever missing? What do all those have to do with anything? How do those affect the deep and weighty issues of life? This is reality, my dear sister. The reality is that no Igbo man is satisfied with just having a female child! You may think Nduka loves you now, but how deep is that love? What happens when his people start to trouble both your lives over a male child to carry on your husband's legacy? You remember how I suffered before Obinna, my first son, saved my life?" she asked me.

"My own in-laws are not like that!" I replied, still struggling to keep my cool.

"Oho! You think you know people! You think you know people until they shock you! And your husband? You had better give him a male child before he gets one outside. He does not even have to know about your intentions to have another child. Accidents happen all the time! Use your tongue to count your teeth, my dear sister! Use your tongue to count your teeth! Use your tongue to count your teeth!" Her words reverberated in my head.

I had had enough! I resolved to ask Nduka to reconsider having a second child as soon as he returned home from work.

"Accidents happen all the time," Obiageli had said.

Indeed, accidents happen all the time because, only a month after I discussed having another child with Nduka, I discovered that I was pregnant! I was shocked to my bones! Yes, I wanted another child! Yes, I had my husband's approval on the matter! Yes, I was happy that I could finally get Obiageli off my back! Yes, I needed another baby to 'save my marriage', as Oby would say, but certainly not now.

While I was happy that Obiageli would let me breathe, I did not think that I could have another child so soon, not with a nine-month-old baby still suckling my breasts. I was not ready; I was not ready at all! I was not done loving Nwakaego yet. How could I have another child? I had hoped I still had a year or two to toy with the idea of becoming 'Mummy-two.' But a month? A month was way too short a time! I wept hysterically that night as I peed on sticks repeatedly, hoping that the result would be different each time.

I was pregnant, for real!

The news that should have filled me with joy weighed me down with sorrow. I wrestled with the idea of embracing motherhood once more, eventually succumbing to its embrace with a heavy heart.

A few weeks after the discovery, I started bleeding profusely. I ordinarily would have been distressed, but I was happy—happy that the baby would go as quickly as it came. I was excited at the thought of going about my business as usual, but two weeks later, the pregnancy symptoms were still as visible as daylight. So, I went for a scan. There was a sac and something within it, to my greatest surprise and delight. Yes, I even listened to the heartbeat of my eight-week-old foetus and knew in my heart that I was carrying a little girl for my Nwakaego.

In that moment, I knew a deep-seated joy had taken root within me. I laughed all the way home, and for the first time in weeks, I admitted to myself that I was genuinely happy about expecting another child. I cannot pinpoint the exact moment she nestled her way into my heart, but nestle in she did, and there she remained, holding onto it with unwavering strength.

A few weeks later, I lifted Nwakaego to my thighs, placed her tiny hands on my tummy, and explained carefully that Mommy was safeguarding her little sister in there, and she would have to leave the breastmilk so her sister would not starve when she came. I felt guilty because Nwakaego was not even up to a year old, but what was I to do? To my delight, my daughter gave me a knowing look and a toothy smile, then struggled to get off my thighs to play with her new doll. From then on, her attention moved from my breasts to my tummy, which she very much enjoyed stroking. I was relieved.

On the weekend, when I became forty-one weeks pregnant, I left my house in the morning for a routine antenatal checkup with Nwakaego in tears. For some inexplicable reason, a wave of sadness washed over me. Nwakaego's tears reminded me of my own when my mother was admitted to the hospital when I was a little girl. Though I did not understand what was wrong with her then, I wept bitterly, as if I already knew she would return to me in a coffin.

Is Nwakaego having such premonitions now? I wondered. I can only trust in the sovereign will of the Lord and ask for His help.

At the clinic, my doctor detained me, and I was admitted for induction because, according to him, I was overdue for labour. I expected to be sent to the theatre, mainly because it had not been two years since I birthed Nwakaego through a caesarean section, but that did not happen. I was instead sent to the ward for cervical ripening that night and induction the following day.

I still recall the excruciating pain I felt that night. Thankfully, I was able to sleep through it.

The following morning, the induction began at a quarter to seven. My contractions went well but began to wane and fail at about noon. Rather than send me to the theatre, which could have saved me all the pain, my oxytocin level was increased, and the induction continued. I cannot explain the pain that I felt, but all the members of the medical team kept saying each time they checked me was, "Two cm."

It soon became a song.

And after several hours, the chorus changed to "Four cm."

Shortly afterwards, a stout doctor came in. "Has your membrane ruptured?" he asked.

That was something I should know, as I could swear I had come across that term in school, but the pain and stress made it difficult to think in the moment.

"I don't know," I replied.

"Has your water broken?"

Oh! Why didn't you just say that at first? "No," I answered.

He began ranting about how younger doctors often gave him unnecessary work and lamented their incompetence. I just lay there, wishing I could push the hands of the clock to when I would hold my baby in my arms.

With the speed of light and now holding a pair of scissors in his right hand, he proceeded to rupture the membrane roughly and angrily.

"If you love your life, you will lie still," he warned. It seemed I was being punished for the sins of the younger doctors.

As soon as the membrane was ruptured and all the water was forced out, my baby stopped kicking! The doctor tried to move the baby forward, but his actions left her locked in my pelvis. At that point, I felt her head obstructing my bladder, and despite being quite pressed, I could not pass urine anymore. After my attending nurse brought me the bedpan for the fourth time and I still could not pass a drop of urine, she walked out on me angrily. She must have felt that I was just craving attention, not knowing how distressed I was.

As the pain intensified, I called out for help, but no one answered. Nduka tried to get them to attend to me, but they told him they could do absolutely nothing because it was labour pains. Oh, Nduka! I felt sorry for him, despite myself. He looked like he had lost fifty kilogrammes overnight. His eyes were pale and hollow, and his otherwise rosy cheeks looked bony. I watched him from the corner of my eye and saw that his hands were shaky and sweaty. I knew then that he was suffering nearly as much as I was. He dashed out again to see if anyone could help us, but I knew it was pointless. I had been given pain relievers twice, but they did not bring any relief.

When the otherwise busy teaching hospital started to feel lonely, a fiery-looking female doctor walked in, grabbed my legs, and swiped me. Oh no! The pain exploded in my head. In tears, I pleaded with her to stop, but she yelled at me that they were trying to help me, and the least I could do was to be grateful and cooperate with them. She asked if I knew how many other patients she had to attend to. I did not think the question needed a reply, so I just continued groaning in pain. I thought of suggesting a simple caesarean section to the lady, but a look into her mean eyes made me kill the thought.

Pressed, thirsty, and dehydrated, I began to feel the pain along my last surgery line, like it was going to burst open. Fortunately, a young house officer stood at the door to my delivery room. He kept looking at me with worry in his eyes. When he could not bear it anymore, he walked in and flipped off the drip. The pain was nonstop, yet I was only six centimetres dilated.

It took about ten minutes for the pain to start easing, but the resident who ruptured the membrane returned and started barking at the house officer. He told him he should have just reduced the flow since he observed that I was in too much pain and did not have to turn off the drip. As the frequency of the contractions reduced, I thankfully began to doze off.

About an hour later, I opened my eyes to find a familiar face looking down at me. It was a childhood friend. The last time I saw him was when we were still students at the University of Nsukka. I was so glad to see him clothed in a medical lab coat at such a distressing time. He, too, was surprised and happy to see me; he came to check up on me since he was told that I was seven centimetres dilated. He checked, insisted that I was still only six centimetres dilated, and advised them to send me to the theatre. I asked him if that was it. He said it was not his decision to make as he was not on the team of doctors assigned to my case.

About ten minutes later, my consultant walked in for the first time since I went into labour. I was unhappy to see him. I told him that I was in too much pain. He asked to examine me, but I complained about the pain again. He apologised and told me he would stop checking when I felt too much pain. Then, he confirmed what my friend had advised and instructed the nurses to prepare me for the theatre.

At this point, it was half past six in the evening. I requested a catheter because my bladder felt extremely heavy, as if it carried ten large gallons of water in it. They told me I would get one in the theatre, but I insisted on getting one there in the labour ward. When they finally fixed it, the tube refused to go in. They had to push hard before they could succeed. It was then that they realised that I had so much urine to pass.

As I got a little relief, I focused on the foetal monitor. I did not know much about the equipment, but something felt off as it counted to one hundred and forty only to drop to eighty, yet the doctors with me paid no attention to it. Perhaps it was nothing to worry about; I really did not know for sure. Exhausted, I must have drifted off to sleep because the doctors woke me up to transfer me to the theatre.

I looked at the digital clock in the room and was shocked to find it was already nine thirty-five at night. I was fatigued beyond words, so I closed my eyes and drifted off to sleep. Thankfully, the pain had subsided a little.

My surgery began at precisely ten that night. I felt numb after being given spinal anaesthesia and chilled to the bone on the operating table, as if submerged in a frozen lake. When I complained, the anaesthesiologist told me he would give me something for the cold after my baby was brought out. My heart skipped a beat when I saw the stout doctor who nearly killed me in the name of rupturing the membrane walk in.

How could they allow such an unkind person in here?

I wanted to complain, but I quickly sucked the words back in. If I complained about 'one of their own' when I was at their mercy, would they let me leave this table with my life? I stayed calm, pulled one of the nurses close, and whispered in her ears.

"Please, ask my husband to give you my rosary to bring to me." She tried to argue that personal items were not allowed in the operating room, but I would not entertain her objections. Yes, it is in moments like this, when you are torn between life and death, that you cling to whatever sovereign being you believe in. As a staunch Catholic, I needed my rosary. Moments later, the nurse brought in the white rosary and helped me place it on my chest.

The doctors, about four of them, were all excited as they chatted about my surgery being the last for the night. One could not wait to catch the match between 'the Red Devils and the Blues'. He teased another doctor that his team would 'finish them off tonight'! While they argued whether the Reds would win or the Blues were more formidable, I noticed that the nurses did not arrange the surgical tools but left them scattered in a metal bowl. The clanging of metal as they searched frantically for what they needed was deafening. I prayed fervently, as if I had recited thirty decades of the rosary. I was that terrified!

An argument ensued between a doctor and a nurse. The doctor wanted an instrument, and the nurse insisted that that instrument did not come with the CS pack. After much ruckus, the doctor used the one the nurse offered while insisting that the one he wanted was longer than the one he was given.

"You see what you made me do?!" I heard him yell a few minutes later.

My heart jumped right out of my chest! What?! What?! What did she make him do? The way the doctor barked and the strain in his voice sounded like he had just declared my end and that of my unborn child.

I closed my eyes to sleep, as I was depleted. After a long while, I woke up to realise that they were still pulling at my baby. I had Nwakaego through a caesarean section. I never imagined it could be such a herculean task to cut open a stomach to get a baby out. I heard loud shouts repeatedly.

"Put your hand here!"

"Pull!"

"Pull!"

"Pull!"

"The baby is not coming!"

"PULL!"

While I was being pulled at so violently, I felt freezing cold. My teeth chattered, and I felt myself shiver despite the numbness. Again, I closed my eyes and prayed five more decades of the rosary. I also prayed for my child that she would have no broken bones. As a girl, how would she survive in a world that places so much emphasis on external beauty? How would she cope with a broken arm, leg, or both? Tears started streaming down my face as I remembered one of my coursemates back at the university. During her birth, the nurse on duty broke her left leg, and now, pretty Chidera still suffers from low self-esteem, which has affected her relationships with men. Chidera is still unmarried, and I am sure her broken leg has much to do with it. How could I lay back helplessly and let my daughter suffer the same fate? I prayed five more decades of my rosary!

I soon started to hear my name from an awfully distant place, but I was in no mood to speak to anyone. I was praying for my child and needed no distractions, but the anaesthesiologist kept on screaming my name! Eventually, I opened my eyes to see his face very close to mine, but he sounded as if he were a planet away.

He asked if I could hear him and see him.

I replied in the affirmative.

He asked if I was dizzy.

I did not think that I was. "No," I answered.

I closed my eyes yet again, and after a while, I was called, and the same questions were asked over and over again.

I knew then that I was dying, but I struggled to keep my eyes open so the doctors would not panic. I ultimately gave up on myself; all my hopes were now placed on my child.

The brightly lit theatre had momentarily become pitch black, and I had lost peripheral vision. The only light I could see was on the machine right in front of me, and though I felt the turbulence beyond the screen, I was as calm as spring waters deep within.

In that darkness, I noticed the doctors had pulled the drips off their stands and were simply squeezing them into my veins at the instructions of the anaesthesiologist.

Suddenly, it felt like a heavy lid had been placed over my nostrils because I could no longer breathe through my nose. I quickly opened my mouth to take in as much air as I could so that my baby would not lack oxygen. I whispered to the doctor closest to me that I could not breathe. He requested oxygen and gave it to me through two tiny nose pipes. One of the doctors standing by my left, who was looking into my open body, commented on the terrible cut I had been given, while two other doctors were in tears.

It was chaotic! The obstetrician called for someone to clean his face because sweat had entered his eyes and he could no longer see. This continued until he got so confused that he shouted for an O&G specialist. Then he called for the consultant assigned to me, who had long gone home by now.

Once again, I could not breathe, so the pipes were exchanged for a mask.

A long time passed before I heard my little girl's weak cry. I rejoiced in my heart that she had survived it all. Oh! How I rejoiced! She did not cry much, nor was she stillborn, but she passed out almost immediately. When they showed her to me, she looked pale. In fact, she was as white as wool. I commented on her fairness and wondered if she had any blood in her at all. I called her by her name, Chidinma, and was delighted to see her. I blessed the Lord for her, but my life was still hanging in the balance.

The obstetrician requested two pints of blood, and I informed them that I was O-. At this point, the doctors and nurses began to scream and run around. Before this time, I did not know I was bleeding or how much blood I had lost.

A doctor returned and confirmed that there was no blood in the blood bank, so Nduka was sent off to search for medicine to stop the bleeding. The bleeding did stop after I took the medicine. What we all did not know at the time was that the medication probably failed because my uterus was not contracted, and the bleeding only stopped because I had run out of blood. The doctors said it was a great miracle that I was still alive and talking, even without blood. I shook my head and prayed more decades.

I reminded the anaesthesiologist about his promise to give me something for the cold after the baby was brought out, but he said he dared not give me anything at that point. Instead, he placed hot bags on my body, which meant nothing to me. I knew they were hot, but they made no difference as I was still as cold as ice. One of the bags scalded my neck, and I began to hover. I told a doctor I was hovering, and he held my hand. I committed my soul to the Lord, for I knew the end had come.

Oh no! I was dying! I was dying, and Nduka would never know what happened to me in here. No one would hear my story. No one would know I had been butchered—sliced apart by the hands of my countrymen, who were entrusted to safeguard my well-being—hacked apart by a system that turns a blind eye to the suffering of its own people, leaving me to bleed out on the altar of recklessness. My spirit hovered over my slaughter bed, and I shook my head in pity.

From a distant place, I heard one of the doctors screaming for me to lift my tongue. I could not understand what he was saying, but he would not let me be, so I stuck out my tongue instead. By this time, I could no longer interpret the things I heard. It felt like I had left the world, and all the nonsense in it no longer concerned me.

Just as I gave up completely and looked forward to reaching another plane, I heard that blood had arrived. According to them, my husband had managed to get the last four pints of O-negative blood left in the blood bank.

So, the blood bank had blood after all, but I was to die and resurrect first before I was given some.

Knowing the country I lived in, I knew Nduka must have tipped everyone, including the dust the blood bank staff walked on, to be given 'all they had'. That, and as I will later hear, he promised to return the blood to them the next day. Whatever got them to change their minds, I was immensely grateful that there was still hope of holding my newborn in my arms, cuddling her, nursing her, and seeing her first smile and first step. Tears of joy streamed down my face, but not for long!

The transfusion began, and the bleeding resumed.

"The uterus is not contracted," the doctors sang as they loosened my stitches afresh. The anaesthesia must have worn off because I felt every bite of the pain.

I cannot say how much time passed, but it soon struck me that the theatre had become as quiet as a graveyard. I asked the anaesthesiologist if I could sleep. After he said, "Yes," I shut my eyes and waited for death to come.

I drifted off to a riverbank, not knowing how I had arrived there. I was in a long queue waiting to be ferried across the river. On either side of the queue were cacti—gigantic cacti! There were cacti everywhere I looked!

What strange place is this, and how did I get here?

I stepped out of the queue for a while because my curiosity got the better of me, and I wanted to see how many people needed to be ferried before it would get to my turn. I was shocked that millions were standing before me and millions more were behind me. There were millions of naked women and babies; some women were standing alone, some babies were standing alone, and some other women clung to their babies like twin pods. I looked at myself; I was naked, too.

I ran to and fro the line, as far as my legs could carry, searching for at least a familiar face in the crowd. I found one!

Bisi Abioye!

Naked Bisi was holding on to her child! Bisi died about a week ago, just right after childbirth. We were roommates at the university and had managed to stay friends until last week, when I was informed by her husband of her tragic demise. You see, Bisi had used a private hospital for her antenatal care and delivery. Unfortunately, there were complications during the delivery—complications too much for the private hospital to handle as they lacked the required facilities. Her baby boy could not breathe on his own, so they hooked him up to oxygen in a van to transport him to the teaching hospital—the last resort for private hospitals. Mid-trip, the oxygen tank emptied, but none of the medical staff noticed until the baby had already died.

Upon hearing the news of her son's death, Bisi went after him.

She could not bear to lose her only child after having prayed earnestly for one for seven long years. Here she was now, clinging to her child as if she feared he could be taken away from her again. I remembered then that Bisi's tragic incident had helped me decide to overlook the unbearable queues at the teaching hospital and have my own child there. Yet, here I was, too.

About a hundred people away from her, I saw a baby with the face of one of my friends, Ivie. Ivie's baby died in the womb due to anoxia caused by a nuchal cord, which the doctors did not detect despite several scans conducted. Ivie still had to go through the horror of pushing out her dead child. My friend lived, but her world became a broken glass that could never be whole again, no matter how hard anyone tried. If only I could tell her now that I saw her baby; if only.

Up the line was Mama Ngozi, our neighbour, who was a schoolteacher. She was clutching her five-kilogramme baby to her chest like a paperweight. She had hoped she would have a caesarean section on the night she went into labour because of the weight of her child, but the doctors told her vaginal delivery was not a problem at all. Now, here she was—*no problem at all!*

"Fall in line! Fall in line!" I heard the ferryman scream at me.

As I turned around quickly, scanning the line to find my place in the queue, I began to hear the feeble cry of my baby. Oh God! No! What is she doing here? I alone should be enough for this place. There is no way I will let my child join me here!

"My baby! My baby! My baby!" I kept screaming as I jolted awake.

I saw a nurse pull the oxygen mask from my face.

"The oxygen is finished!" she exclaimed.

I greeted her even as tears strolled down my face freely. When she asked the reason for my tears, I told her I was glad to be alive. I asked for my baby and was told she was in the neonatal ward. I asked to see her but was told I could not. Then, I pleaded with the nurse to help me check up on her. The nurse did not return until nearly an hour later—the longest one hour of my life. I saw her return, distressed and in tears. My heart left my chest momentarily as I remembered my dream.

"What is it? How's my baby? Where's my baby?" I asked her. I tried to get up, but the pain sent a billion waves through my head. The nurse just kept crying until my anxiety and frustration turned into anger. "Where's my baby?!" I screamed impatiently.

"My sister," she started, shaking her head pitifully. "God is really on your side! That time you told me to check up on your baby ehn, as soon as I got there, she had turned blue from lack of oxygen. It was when I got there that I quickly alerted the doctors. Hmmm! But she's fine now, sha."

I could not express how delighted I was, though I was still far from being out of the woods myself. Later, I was informed that my brother had come to donate blood at about one in the morning, but that did not stop me from gasping for air. It was a nightmare to deal with, but I was not placed on oxygen. The hospital was out of oxygen.

I remained in the recovery room for two days, two torturous days where the women at the riverbank took turns to pay me a visit each time I closed my eyes.

"Do you know what got me to the riverbank?" One of them asked me. "Power failure!" she answered her own question. "I was in the theatre, trying to have my third baby, when darkness spread its black cloak around the room. The doctors quickly lit the candles they had brought in as part of their working tools, like they knew this would happen. There I was on the operating table with nurses holding candles over my open body, and one doctor accidentally slit an artery, and boom! I was blown away to the riverbank, waiting to be ferried away. My baby miraculously lived, but I was gone, yet no one knows what they did to me."

Before she was done, another woman strolled in with her baby.

"Yours is even good," she said. "I died with my baby. My pelvis was too narrow for a normal delivery, but my husband said he would not have it any other way. He insisted that I use the hospital he chose for my delivery—a hospital where the staff, like him, strongly believed in only vaginal deliveries. Now, I am stuck at the riverbank. The doctors have long forgotten they ever met me, and my husband's new wife is pregnant," she lamented.

"I tell you, all the good doctors in the country have moved to greener pastures. What we have left are a few good ones, overworked to their bones, and plenty of those who slept through medical school," a third woman cried.

"Why would they not sleep?" a fourth interjected. "Every month, strike! Strike! Strike! Each time they go on strike like that, they forget what they learned before. Besides, everyday theory! Theory! Some of them never do any real practical work until they are staring at our open bodies on the table. And again, do they have the equipment needed for their training? Are our academic institutions funded adequately? Who will pay for extensive research when we are all struggling to survive? Don't blame the doctors; blame our bloated politicians," she concluded.

"One night, the black goat will run wildly into the marketplace, and its hooves will tap out a deadly tune on the dusty ground. As it disappears into the evil forest, never to be seen or heard from again, the people's rejoicing will be so loud it will make its ears bleed! One day, when desperation sets in and hunger begins to chew at its belly, the dog will see its master for the demon he truly is and will bare its teeth like sharp knives under the watchful gaze of the moon. It will pounce on its own master, tear apart the flesh it once served, leave the remains for vultures to feast on, and completely break the bond of loyalty," a fifth woman proclaimed with wildfire blazing in her eyes.

"Speak up! Speak up! Speak up!" the thousands of women who had now filled my hospital room were all chanting. I jerked awake, sweating profusely, and for several months after that, the thought of shutting my eyes even for a minute became a very horrible nightmare.

The doctors wrote that I had lost three litres of blood, which was the reason for the complication. They had to cover up their tracks.

"Speak up!" the women continuously chanted. "Speak up!" they always cried.

Could this be what they meant? For me to sing like a canary about my horrible treatment on the surgical slab? I wondered.

My consultant came the next day and complained bitterly about the delay in carrying out his directive for surgery scheduled for half past six the evening before. However, his ranting felt like 'medicine after death' to me. How could he go home to sleep—and perhaps have a pleasant time with his wife—while I was in such a precarious situation?

"Speak up!" I heard loud and clear again.

My little girl was brought to me on the fifth day. She had been transfused, and we were discharged to go home after she completed her medicines. Meanwhile, I was sent home with open and infected wounds, which only healed after four harrowing weeks. For five long weeks, I felt dizzy, but I eventually resumed my bustling routine. I was informed that I had suffered a cardiac arrest in the theatre, causing all my vital signs to disappear from the monitor. It was an unexplainable mystery to the doctors how I survived.

"Madam, people don't survive what you survived," one of them said when he came to see me two days after the delivery.

About a month after I left the hospital, I inquired about the procedure for reporting errant doctors in a government hospital. I was told not to bother, as doctors protect their own. And if I was willing to pursue a lengthy case with them, the most they would do to the doctors would be to suspend their medical licences for six months, after which it would be business as usual. I had to consider whether that was punishment enough to make lifelong enemies, especially since I had no strength left in me to put up a fight. You see, we Nigerians forgive quickly. We forgive our politicians for every sin that sends us to the slaughterhouse time and again. We forgive our schools when our children die under their care while they slumber. We forgive the drunk driver who takes our loved ones from us with one careless move. We forgive the trigger-happy police when their bullets strike us in the chest, though we are blameless. We forgive incompetence at all levels, so much so that incompetence has become a leviathan, demanding forgiveness with vehemence.

The road to recovery was a long and distressing one. I suffered physically, emotionally, and psychologically for a prolonged period. The headaches persisted, as if someone were following me around, relentlessly striking my head with a sledgehammer. Perhaps the nightmares and hallucinations contributed to this torment. Yes, the women continued to come to me, urging me to share their stories. I only began to find peace within my spirit when I started to write down the events.

As for my little girl, she suffered from seizures for a long time. It was so severe that I feared the worst, but I am grateful she is almost past it now. I was informed that choking and seizures are common for a resuscitated baby. Every day, I watch her follow her older sister around like a shadow, and then, I take a deep breath.

I am grateful.

My babies are each other's companions in this harsh, cold world, and my heart leaps with joy every time I hear them whispering and giggling.

***

For several months after I left the hospital, I could barely speak. Nduka kept asking what had happened in the theatre, but I remained silent. It was not that I did not want to tell him. In fact, I was eager to share my story, but the words always seemed to get stuck in my throat whenever I tried to speak. Thankfully, he was patient and understanding—more than that, he was everything I could have ever hoped for.

On the night little Chidinma turned one, he pulled me into our room away from the small crowd gathered to celebrate our daughter, and handed me a document. As soon as I read it, tears welled up in my eyes. I looked at Nduka as if I were seeing him for the first time since my delivery. I could not believe how fortunate I was to have such a kind man as my husband.

"Nduka, are you sure?" I asked anxiously.

He kissed me softly on my right cheek and said he was sure.

"What if…"

"No what-ifs," he interrupted, and I burst into tears. "I don't know what happened in that theatre, Nkem, but please try to put your mind at ease because it won't happen again," he said, as I rushed into his arms, crying hysterically.

***

Obiageli visited me two months after Chidinma's first birthday, bringing with her the usual boy-child madness. I did not tell her about my ordeal at the hospital, but I am sure she heard bits and pieces from Nduka and our brother. It beats me how anyone could be so insensitive. She started asking when I planned to give Chidinma a younger brother, as if she were my fertility alarm clock.

Next, she dabbled into how my daughters amounted to nothing in my husband's and his family's eyes, and how Nduka might seek a male child outside the marriage if I could not overcome my past, summon courage, and give him one. I did not say a word, but I gave her a cold stare that made her swallow the remaining words she had in her mouth.

Handing me the document that showed he had undergone a vasectomy had dispelled all doubts in my mind about the value of my daughters to Nduka. It also reinforced my confidence in his love for me and my importance in his life.

Since then, it felt as though a huge rock had been lifted off my shoulders, as if I had been given a million more years to live. I no longer needed to hide in the shadows, fearing the next 'accident' that might force me back to the slaughterhouse and the slaughter slab to face the butchers' knives. I felt reborn; I no longer needed to hold off living. I was excited—yes, exhilarated!

I would not have to suffer the same fate as Nnu Ego, whose sole purpose in life was to live and die for her children. I wanted more for myself. I knew I could achieve more; I knew I carried so much potential within me. Now was the best time to stop being so afraid of dying that I never truly lived. After experiencing death, resurrection, and a second chance at life, I would be doing myself a great disservice if I did not enjoy every moment to the fullest.

The following day, I bought two brand-new rosaries for my daughters: Nwakaego received the blue one, while Chidinma got the pink. In my darkest hour, my rosary had brought me comfort and peace, reminding me of a power far beyond the physical. I was now certain that the same power would keep my daughters safe. With that reassurance, I no longer had to worry excessively about them as I enrolled them in a crèche and began searching for schools for myself as well.

Yes, I needed to go back to school. Since I started the restaurant business years ago, I had woven a savings culture into the very fabric of my being. For every kobo I spent on the household, I saved a little more, constantly pinching pennies to ensure there was enough money in the bank to cover all the 'what-ifs' that my mind conjured from time to time. The loudest what-if was: "What if Nduka lost his job and could no longer provide for the family? What would happen to my children?"

It happened to Obiageli's husband. He lost his job with the bottling company years ago, and since then, all he has managed to do is father one malnourished child after another. Obiageli, who could have put her nursing certificate to good use, insists it is not her responsibility to provide for herself or her children. In her view, if she has not failed in her wifely duties, neither should he. Perhaps it was time to turn the tables on her. If she ever brought up the boy-child conversation again, I would silence her by suggesting she get a job and save her family from starvation. That would certainly get her off my back.

About school: I felt a strong need to return to school. Empowering myself further would better equip me to support my children and handle whatever uncertainties life throws our way. My biology degree was no longer sufficient; I had never truly wanted to study it in the first place. Nonetheless, it was better than doing nothing after multiple attempts to gain admission into medical school had failed—one needed the right connections to secure a place. When the opportunity arose to study biology at the University of Nsukka, I seized it eagerly. However, after nearly drifting into the world beyond in that theatre room, an experience that I now view as a call to address the needs of my country and discover my true purpose, I am convinced that my path lies in becoming a well-trained medical doctor. I am determined to ensure that no woman endures what I did, at least not while I am here.

I could be anything I desired. The money I had saved over the years could fund a medical degree abroad and provide me with the expertise needed to return home and care for pregnant women. My wonderful Nduka would be thrilled at the prospect. I had been given a second chance—a second chance at life. Managing a small restaurant was no longer enough. I wanted to be more; I needed to achieve more!

Days melted into nights, weeks into months, and months into years. Yet, my resolve remained unchanged: to never hold off living, to silence all the what-ifs in my head and just take the plunge into life, to enjoy each moment as if it were my last, to sip water as though it were the finest wine, to take time each day to listen to the melodies of birds, to immerse myself in the colours of the things around me as if I were seeing them for the very first time; to kiss Nduka ever so passionately; to listen to the laughter of our children, unburdened by fear; and to watch them spread their wings and soar, flying round and round the large blue sky that is big enough for me to fly too.

The memory of the riverbank occupies my thoughts daily, ceaselessly, like the steady flow of the Nile. The women's visits no longer fill me with dread; they have become my sorority sisters and guiding light as I strive to ensure that no woman or child sets foot on the riverbank ever again.

Thank you for reading! If you enjoyed this book, I would love to hear your thoughts. Your reviews and feedback mean the world to me and help others discover this book. Please take a moment to share your opinion on your favorite review platform, or reach out directly. Your support is greatly appreciated!

Printed in Great Britain
by Amazon

58216932R00098